DECEIVED BY HELL

Erin Bedford

More By Erin Bedford

The Underground Series
Chasing Rabbits
Chasing Cats
Chasing Princes
Chasing Shadows
Chasing Hearts

Fairy Tale Bad Boys
Hunter
Pirate
Thief
Mirror
Stepbrother

The Mary Wiles Chronicles
Marked By Hell
Bound By Hell
Deceived By Hell

Vampire CEO
Until Midnight
Granting Her Wish

The Celestial War Chronicles
Song of Blood and Fire
Visions of War and Water

DECEIVED BY HELL

Erin Bedford

1

THEY SAY THERE IS a special place in hell for lawyers. Now, while I had been to hell myself, I couldn't say one way or another if it was true. I did know Christy Fontanelle was as fierce a lawyer as a dresser.

Clad in fitted trousers and a matching blazer, her fire-truck-red heels a sharp contrast to the black of her suit and her lipstick the same shocking red of her shoes, Christy was able to make the strongest of men quiver in fear of her frown. I wasn't a man. Or human for that matter. So, her laser gaze—which scanned up and down my form—was a wasted effort.

I sat in the witness stand, arms crossed, my foot tapping impatiently—something Christy zeroed in on immediately.

"Nervous, Miss Wiles?" she asked in a husky voice. I'd bet she had all the men in her firm scurrying for her favor. I sure would have had I been interested in women. Alas, the voice I was interested in belonged to the person waiting for me to show up for our first official date.

"Impatient," I shot back not giving any more information than needed.

Her lips ticked up at the edges but the smile didn't meet her eyes. "Well, I'll try to make this as quick as possible. We wouldn't want to inconvenience you while we try to catch a killer. Now would we?"

The utter disdain in her voice didn't faze me. "I'd appreciate it."

Christy's startled expression told me she hadn't expected my response.

Good. I wouldn't want to make this any easier for her.

Thompson—who sat behind the plaintiff's side of the courtroom—huffed audibly. He had never liked to bring me to court; he knew I'd tell the truth no matter how gruesome or unsavory it may be. He'd once tried to ask me to bend my story a bit so we would get a guaranteed conviction, but when I'd refused he'd responded by not talking to me for a month. Thompson, and the rest of the police force, said I was a wild card. I might be a great resource for law enforcement but I could sure make things harder for the good guys. I didn't blame them for any of it. As a former archangel, I was still wired to be honest and seek justice the right way. I was slowly, but surely, learning my angelic ways were naive and pointless in the human world.

It wasn't often I was asked to appear in court for some case or another, but when I did, I always found the experience unpleasant. Today was no different.

The accused, Peter Billings, was a fairly attractive man with light brown hair, green eyes, and an athletic build—probably due to spending more time at the gym than with his wife.

Former wife. I corrected myself.

"Let's get down to the point," Christy said clasping her hands in front of her as she posed for the court. "You were hired by the wife of my client, Peter Billings, to follow him. Correct?"

"Yes." I gave a short nod.

"And what were you hoping to find by following him?" Her head cocked to the side causing her hair to fall across her forehead.

My eyes narrowed. She knew exactly why I had been following him. As a Private Investigator, I mainly handled cases the police had already closed that the family wanted investigated further. Unfortunately, as a former angel, I attracted the weird and supernatural. So, I ended up doing a lot of dispossession and hauntings. But more often than not, most of my cases involved cheating spouses. Peter Billings fell into the last category.

"I didn't hope anything." I shook my head. "But Mrs. Billings believed Mr. Billings was having an affair."

Christy pretended to think on it for a moment and then asked, "So she hired you to take pictures of him with another woman."

"Yes."

My answer made Christy smile, "If you were supposed to be taking pictures of Mr. Billings and another woman, why were you taking photos of him with his wife? Is that part of your job as well, or are you just a Peeping Tom?" The court-room audience laughed and Christy's smile broadened. She had them in the palm of her hand and she knew it.

Not letting her bother me, I explained, "I don't let my clients know when I am going to be taking the photos."

"Why not? Don't you trust your clients?" Christy asked, her tone suggesting I should be the one who wasn't trustworthy.

"To be frank, no." Thompson made another disapproving noise which I promptly ignored. "Humans are too focused on what benefits them. By taking the

11

photos at unscheduled intervals, there is no chance for evidence to be misconstrued." My lips quirked at the sides. "And I highly doubt Mrs. Billings could have predicted her husband would kill her at the exact moment I had chosen to monitor him."

Christy appeared to think on this for a moment before she turned to the jury who had hung on her every word up until this point, "Pictures are a funny thing. So many factors go into making a photograph look just right. The right lighting, the right position," her eyes gleamed as she slid her gaze back over to me, "the right manipulation."

An outcry from the courtroom caused the judge to pound his gavel and request order to resume. I watched Christy without showing the outrage she no doubt hoped for. I was sorry to disappoint her but I wasn't the kind.

"I believe you are suggesting I altered the photographs I took in order to portray Mr. Billings stabbing his wife with a pair of scissors." I gave her a lopsided grin, "I'm sorry to tell you my skills aren't up to par with modern-day technology. I can point a camera and push a button. Anything else and I'm lost." I shrugged and let the issue rest. Unfortunately, Christy didn't.

"So, you are saying your photography skills are not of a professional? Where did you say you went to school Miss Wiles?" the tenacious lawyer asked, but before I could answer raised a finger, "Oh, wait. You didn't. In fact," she turned about the court room, "You don't have any record of going school anywhere. California or otherwise."

"Objection." The district attorney, Michelle Lord, stood to her feet. "I don't see how this has anything to do with the case at hand. Miss Wiles gave us the memory card showing they weren't changed. Mrs. Fontanelle is out of line."

The judge—an elderly woman with kind eyes—nodded, "I agree. Mrs. Fontanelle, if you aren't going to ask anything relevant of the witness then sit down."

"I apologize your honor." Christy's face said she was anything but contrite, and when she turned back to me I just knew she was going to ask something even worse. "Miss Wiles, you also work for the LAPD on occasion. Is this correct?"

"Yes." My back stiffened as I waited for the other shoe to drop.

"And in that time, you've helped them solve so many cases," a false admiration filled her voice, "You must be very proud of yourself."

It wasn't a question, so I didn't answer.

My lack of response didn't seem to bother her because she continued, "I read over your long list of credentials and praises for your work, but there is one thing I just can't understand. Why—if the LAPD does such a fantastic job—do they need the help of someone like you?" she cocked her head to the side and I could see Thompson's face out of the corner of my eye becoming a deeper shade of purple. Christy was not making any friends in the local law enforcement.

Since she had asked a question, I was bound by law to answer it, though I knew why she wanted me to. "I specialize in a certain type of crime."

"Oh, yes," Christy smiled as if remembering something pleasant and then she paused for a moment. She turned to the jury, her voice low as if telling a secret, "You see, Miss Wiles specializes in the occult cases. The creepy, unexplained kind of phenomenon you only hear about in movies."

This caused a rumble of mutters from the jury and crowd. I sat calmly in my seat as the judge once more called order to the courtroom. Some would wonder why my specialization mattered, why Christy would bring it up, but most of us knew the reason.

People didn't like different. They didn't like what they couldn't explain. And Christy had lowered my credibility in the eyes of the jury from stellar to skeptical. I didn't envy the district attorney. She'd have to try and make the jury see beyond my peculiar skills and focus on the evidence. Peter Billings was caught on camera stabbing his wife.

After my part was done and I was able to leave, I met Thompson out in the hallway. He was a large man, not fat by any means but the kind of muscles that came from working out and hard labor. Thompson had once told me his family owned a farm outside of L.A. He'd talked about it with such longing I had wondered why he had come to LA if he missed it so much. But it wasn't any of my business.

"You're pretty dressed up for a court appearance," Thompson asked, his eyes scanning up and down my form.

Normally, I wore jeans and a t-shirt for most occasions, but when I had to appear in court I mixed it up with slacks and a silken shirt. Today, though, I wore an A-line skirt which billowed out around my thighs and a sleeveless top which showed just a hint of cleavage. Trisha had picked the outfit out.

"I have a date now."

Thompson's brows rose at my response and then a sly grin spread across his lips. "A date? Since when you do date?"

Crossing my arms over my chest, I shifted from one leg to the other. "Since now. Not that it is any business of yours."

"Don't get defensive. I was just asking." Thompson held his hands up in defense and then asked, "So, who's the lucky guy?"

"If you must know, it's Sid."

"Magnus?" he cocked a brow, his eyes full of amusement, "You mean the guy who's not your boyfriend?"

I shrugged. "He's still not. That would require some kind of discussion. Or at least that's what Trisha says. For some reason, she believes if a guy gives you an orgasm there must be some kind of talk afterward."

"Woah," Thompson shook his hands and took a step back from me, "That's too much information."

I frowned, my brows scrunching together, "Why? You're married, aren't you?"

"Yeah, but that's beside the point," his eyes searched around us like a scared kitten, "You shouldn't be talking to me about those things."

"What? Sex?" my words echoed in the court hallway, causing a few people to look our way.

"Shh," Thompson hissed, putting his finger up to his lips, "Can't you talk to Trisha about this?"

"Why?" I cocked my head to the side, enjoying his discomfort a bit more than I should have. Humans were so finicky about sex, especially men. Though, I wasn't sure why. They all did it. Shouldn't they be able to talk about it without it getting weird?

"Because you just can't."

I let out an exaggerated sigh. "Well, either way. We can't very well be a couple if I'm the only one who's had an orgasm. I mean shouldn't it be both ways?" I asked to a befuddled Thompson, continuing before he could answer, "I think he has to at least have one too . . . before we can even think about being a mated pair."

"Mated pair?" confusion covered Thompson's face but then he shook his head, "Look, I don't know what kind of things you are into but it sounds like something you should be talking about with him and not . . . well not me." The sergeant walked away without waiting for me to respond.

Watching his back as he walked away I couldn't help but smirk. It wasn't often I was able to fluster Thompson. Now that I knew this particular topic bothered him, I would have to remember to use it more in the future. Just to keep him on his toes.

After Thompson left, the court room doors opened and the occupants spilled out. Among them was none other than Christy Fontanelle. Her eyes on her phone, she must have felt me watching because her gaze shot up to meet mine. A slow smile spread across her lips as she changed her trajectory.

"Miss Wiles," she greeted without offering me her hand.

"Mrs. Fontanelle."

"I hope I didn't ruffle too many feathers back there." She pointed a thumb back the court room.

"You were just doing your job," I commented with a shrug.

"Right," her smile brightened further, "In any case, I hope after this is all said and done you might be willing to speak with me about some of your other cases. The occult has always fascinated me and I even did a philosophy paper about it back in college."

"Really?" I asked, not at all interested but knowing it was the answer she expected.

"Yes! It was about the demons and their existence in our world. I'd love to get your insights on the subject."

Not wanting to create more trouble for myself, I gave her a tight smile, "Sure. Give me your card and I'll give you a call."

I could see the excitement in her face as she dug around for a card and I almost felt bad for her. I had no intention of calling her, or having any such chat. I was in the business of putting demons down. It had more to do with guns and what people might call magic than philosophical discussions.

"Here," she handed me the card, "I have to get going but I hope to hear from you soon."

"Bye," I waved the card in the air as she turned her back on me. When she was around the corner, I crumbled the card in my hand before tossing it in the trash.

Christy Fontanelle wasn't interested in talking to me about demons. If I'd learned anything from today it was that Christy didn't play by the rules. It was probably one of the reason's Mr. Billings had hired her.

A shark in Prada; the moment I had seen her I had dropped the veil on my powers and read her soul. Like most people, she had murky bits but deep in her heart was a dark spot which would eventually grow out of control if she didn't take care.

Not that I could do anything about it. I wasn't there to save her. Or anyone else for that matter. The only person I was worried about was currently back in my office probably being driven up the wall by my assistant.

2

MY COURT APPEARANCE HAD been at three and my date was supposed to be at four, but on my way there Sid had called telling me he was running late and had asked if we could reschedule to five. Since I had no intention of waiting around like some love-sick fool, I headed back to the office to check on my new guest.

As I walked through the front door, I was surprised to find my assistant-slash-hacker-on-demand— Trisha—sitting at her desk. Her naturally blonde hair was colored black and was pulled up into a bun. She usually wore pink streaks in her hair, but today she had opted for blue, probably to match the color of the corset top she wore.

Trisha's style was what she liked to call alternative. One time someone had called her gothic and she had almost blown a gasket—not that I really knew the difference. They were all peculiar to me. We didn't have different styles of clothing in heaven. We all wore the same clothing issued by the higher-ups.

I sighed to myself. Those were the days.

"How was court?" Trisha asked when she saw me.

Tossing the car keys onto her desk, I shrugged, "The usual."

"And my baby?" Trisha picked the keys up and quirked a thin brow.

"Fine. Not a scratch on her."

I had only recently learned how to drive, and had yet to get my own vehicle. Since I usually had Trisha cart me around, she had graciously allowed me to use her vehicle while I was at court and she babysat. Thinking of my house guest caused my gaze to turn from my assistant to the office door—which was closed.

"How is he?"

Trisha's blue eyes followed my gaze and she frowned. She didn't ask who I was talking about. We both knew the only he in this building was my former commander and fellow angel, Ramiel. For the last five years, I'd been searching both for him as well as the wings which had been taken from me. Fortunately enough, I had found him. Only I hadn't found my wings. I didn't even want to get into what it had cost me to find him.

"He's been in there since you left. I tried to start a conversation with him but he didn't have much to say. He's not very polite." She gave me a pointed look.

"I wouldn't expect so. Not after all he's been through. Though," I paused in thought, "I don't remember him being too cheerful back in heaven either. He was my commander and I had looked up to him, though I hadn't exactly tried to have polite conversation."

"Still," Trisha threw her tights-clad legs up on the table and rocked back in her chair, "You'd think the guy could learn some people skills or something. I mean, yeah sure, he had been tortured by demons but so were you and you aren't all doom and gloom." She gestured at hand at me and I rolled my eyes.

"Gee, thanks."

"You know what I mean, Mare."

"Yeah, I do," I reassured her before moving from the table and toward the office door. I paused with my hand on the door knob and was about to push it open but I heard voices through the door. Frowning, I leaned forward to press my ear against the door.

The voices were muffled but I was sure Ramiel was talking to someone. My hand went to the door handle and without warning, I turned the knob and threw open the door.

Ramiel looked up the moment I stepped across the threshold. He had my desk phone to his ear and a pensive look on his face. He muttered something into the phone before hanging it up.

"Muriel." Ramiel stood from my desk and greeted me with open arms. I didn't step into his embrace. I tried not to touch Ramiel too often. Each time contact with him caused a sick feeling in my stomach which I was determined to ignore for now.

So, instead, I bypassed him for the mini fridge I kept in the room. The office also acted as my bedroom and kitchen. As a former archangel, I didn't have much care for worldly possessions, so the place worked well enough for me.

"I've told you before, it's Mary down here," I tried to keep the irritation out of my voice. I didn't know why I cared what he thought—he wasn't my commander any more. If anything, he was less than me. I shook the thought from my mind before my disgust ended up showing on my face.

"My apologies," Ramiel's brow furrowed and then his eyes scanned my clothing, "I thought you were meeting someone? At least, that is what the little girl out there kept telling me."

"She's not a little girl," I snapped, becoming defensive, "Trisha is my assistant and one of my best friends since coming to earth."

"A little girl none the less," Ramiel stated, disdain on his face, "And a human. We are angelic beings. We do not befriend humans."

It was an argument we'd had on more than one occasion since he had come to stay with me. One in which I had been exceedingly tempted to end with a bullet to his head. Only sheer curiosity—and the need to know what exactly he was up to on earth—kept me from turning his butt out into the cold.

See, there was one startling difference between Ramiel and me. One I still was trying to deny, but didn't think I could for much longer. While I had had my wings taken from me by demons in an attempt to save Ramiel's sorry ass, he had willingly given his up. A fact I had only recently discovered on my own, and one which I had yet to bringing myself to confront him about.

"Anyways," I changed the subject, "I did have somewhere to go after court but there was a delay, so I decided to come see how you were doing."

Ramiel's expression softened as he took a step toward me. I forced myself not to back away from him as he placed his hands on my shoulders. Bile threatened to rise in my throat and I pushed it back down. One of the telltale signs of a fallen angel was the distinct lack of God's holy presence, as well as the stink of evil. Demons gave off the same kind of presence, at least, when they were veiling it.

"I have missed you, Muriel," he pressed my head to his chest, his own height a foot taller than mine. I didn't bother to correct him on my name again, the strength it took for me to stay still taking precedence.

Not seeming to notice my discomfort he stroked the back of my head and murmured, "I had often dreamed of us being like this. Together with no ranks or rules to hold us back."

This caused me to jerk away. It was the first I had heard of it. Since Ramiel had come to stay with me he had pretty much kept to himself. He'd refused to talk about what had happened to him any further and when pressed would try and use his former rank against me. I hadn't pressed too much, hoping he would come forward on his own, but this was different.

"I had too," I admitted and took a step back as he smiled, "Once. But not anymore."

His smile fell.

A smart person would have played along to get more information out of him, but it just didn't feel right to me. If I had been unattached I would have gladly played the decoy; I'd done it before. But seeing as Sid and I had recently kindled an arrangement of sorts, I didn't think it would be right to pretend with someone else until I knew the rules.

And humans were all about rules. Sid maybe half demon but he was half human too. From my experience with Trisha he would not appreciate me hanging around another guy without having discussed it with him first. Whatever it was.

Probably something to do with why I had to be all dressed up to have a meal with the half-demon.

"What has changed?" he asked, trying to take me in his arms once more, "Is it because of your lost wings?"

His mention of my wings caused the scars on my back to twinge. I still had nightmares of my time in hell. The sound of metal against bone, my throat burning from the screams, and the ever-present prayer for someone to help me. No one had ever come, though. In the end, it had been me who had escaped. Though, the how was still a bit murky.

I remembered my cell door being left open, and I remembered dragging myself down a stone corridor which had ended in a portal opening to the human world. Whether my cell door had been left open by mistake or on purpose, I had never found out, and doubted I ever would.

Shaking my head of the memories, I maneuvered around Ramiel and back toward the office door, "It's more than that. Things have changed. I've changed," I paused with my hand on the frame of the door, my gaze on the ground, "I'm not the same subservient creature who will blindly follow orders."

"I never thought you were," Ramiel tried to argue, but I kept going.

"Yes, you did. And you still do. Or you wouldn't expect me to just take your word for it without question," I didn't elaborate on what it was—we'd had this conversation before. He knew very well what I was talking about. His story didn't add up and I wanted answers, whether he liked it or not. I was quiet for a moment and then said, "I won't be kept in the dark. Not anymore."

3

SID AND I HAD agreed to meet at Gianni's for an early dinner since he had to be at the bar he owned— The Night Owl—to work the evening shift. Unfortunately, our early dinner had been shifted to a later one since by time I arrived there was an hour wait.

"Do you want to go somewhere else?" I turned to him after the hostess told us the wait time.

Sid's brows furrowed and a frown marred his beautiful lips. Bar-owner, and the son of the demon of lust, Sid had a certain bad-boy presence about him, which made even the older women in the waiting room sneak glances his way. As an angel, I never really paid much mind to the attractiveness of others, Except for Sid. He'd always been the exception, even before I'd known I was attracted to him.

Not that anyone would blame me. Dark hair fell over his eyes in a boyish way which became a lethal combination when his long lashes blinked your way. Even now, I had a hard time keeping my hands to my sides, the urge to touch him was so great.

He pulled his lower lip into his mouth and chewed on it for a moment, causing things low inside of me to tighten. His nostrils flared, the worry in his eyes changing to heated. The want in it so strong I felt it zing down my skin, pulling a gasp from me.

Did I mention one of Sid's abilities included being able to sense desire? Yeah, and he had a whole demon side of him which needed to feed on those emotions. A fact which I'd recently learned when I'd experienced my first human phenomenon. An orgasm.

Just thinking about our last time together in his truck and the rippling overwhelming affect he'd had on me, made the feeling heighten. Sid grasped me by the waist and pulled me to him. At least, I wasn't the only one affected. The bulge in the front of his pants pressed against my hips. I knew we were drawing the attention of the occupants of the waiting area but I couldn't find the need to care.

"Sidney," I murmured, his thumb caressing along the edge of my jaw line. I turned my face into his hand, my lips brushing his hand.

Sid let out a shaky breath and then slowly dropped his and stepped back from me. The corners of my lips turned down as I took in deep breaths.

"No," after a moment Sid finally said, "I want us to go on a date, a real date. I don't want this to be some physical thing."

I cocked my head to the side and slowly drew out, "Okay. Is this the talk?"

"The talk?" his brows rose and his lips ticked up at the corners.

I glanced around us and my eyes met with those of the watching restaurant occupants. "Maybe we should go somewhere else for this?"

Sid pushed up the sleeve of his long-sleeved tight-fitted shirt to glance at his watch. "Yeah, I don't think we are going to make dinner here tonight. Peggy's?"

"Sounds good," I followed him out of the restaurant and into the parking lot. "Should I just follow you?" I glanced to Trisha's car and then to his large truck.

"Nah, you're on my way back. I'll just drop you off on the way to the bar." He pulled his keys out of his pocket and I admired the way his pants clung to his backside as he made his way to the driver's side.

I climbed into the passenger seat beside him and shut the door. My gaze scanned the interior of the vehicle. This had been where we had done it. Or well, I had done it. Sid had been doing all the giving, I'd just been along for the ride.

"Don't." The stern sound of Sid's voice pulled me out of my thoughts.

"What?" I asked, my gaze turning to him. His eyes were focused in front of him, his hands clenching the steering wheel until his knuckles turned white.

"I'm holding on by a thread here, angel. If you keep smelling like that the whole time, I don't think we'll make it to dinner, let alone desert." He shot me tortured look before turning his eyes back to the front of the car.

Frowning hard, I asked, "Didn't you feed today?"

"Yes," he sighed and raked a hand through his hair, "But it seems like I need more lately. A lot more. Ever since..."

He trailed off and I finished for him, "Since your father came through from the portal."

To save Ramiel I'd had to make a deal with a demon lord—Sid's father to be exact. Asmodeus, the demon of lust, had wanted me to open the portal to hell using Michael's blade so he could cross over. When he'd given me the deal I should have shoved it right up his ass. I wasn't surprised his being here on earth was affecting Sid's powers. I just hoped there weren't any other repercussions for my mistake.

"Yeah," Sid breathed out heavily. I turned my attention away from the strained look on his face and tried to think of something else. Anything else. As long as it wasn't remotely sexual.

Cheating spouses, Christy's smug face this morning. That was good. The only emotion the woman initiated in me was caution. Hopefully, Thompson and the defense attorney felt the same way or Mrs. Billings murder would go unpunished. I wished there was something I could do further to help but other than the photographs—which showed blatant proof of Peter's guilt—I had nothing. It wasn't as though her ghost was going to show up and show me where the murder weapon was hidden.

My line of thought must have helped because Sid shifted his truck out of park and pull out of the parking lot of Gianni's. The air was thick with tension as we headed down the street. We both seemed afraid of causing Sid another break down.

"How's what's-his-face?" Sid said after a moment, his eyes glancing over to me.

I frowned. He knew very well what Ramiel's name was, but ever since my ex-commander had begun staying with me, Sid had refused to mention him by name. Preferring to use terms like 'that guy' or 'the other angel.' It made me wonder if Sid was jealous—which was ridiculous Sid didn't seem the type—but stranger things have happened.

"He's fine. Still not talking though." I'd told Sid about Ramiel's explanation as to how he had gotten away from the demons and why he hadn't tried to find me in the whole five years I'd been in the human world. Sid had found it unbelievable as well. What I hadn't told him though was about my suspicions of Ramiel's falling. I only had my own eyes and feelings to go off of and I didn't want to worry Sid further than needed. Knowing how protective Sid has become of me lately, he'd probably try to get Ramiel out of my house.

"You shouldn't trust him. Not until we know for sure what side he's on," Sid cast me a sideways warning glance, "My father is a tricky bastard and could be using him to get to you."

I shook my head and said, "I don't know what else he could possibly want from me. He's already crossed over to this side."

Sid snickered, "Yeah, but he's powerless thanks to you."

"Not completely," I pointed out, "He still had some power, and the charm only suppressed his more violent ones."

"Exactly. Which is why he is still so focused on you. While I might have put the talisman on him, only someone like you can take it off."

"Someone like me?" my brows furrowed as I stared hard at the dashboard.

"You know, an archangel," Sid waved a hand at me, "That thing is meant to suppress demon powers I highly doubt I, or any other demon, could even touch it while it's active, let alone take it off."

The talisman—made of animal bones—had been created by my landlord Madame Serena. She owned the wiccan shop below my office, and up until recently had just been the crazy woman downstairs. It wasn't until my friend Adara, an ex-demon hunter, had brought her in to help me tame Asmodeus that I found out she had known about me all along. Madame Serena hadn't told me everything about the charm. I only knew it would weaken Asmodeus enough so he wouldn't be a threat in the human world. But Asmodeus would never be completely powerless. He'd always find some way to get what he wanted, and he didn't care who stood in his way to do it.

Sid pulled into the parking lot of Peggy's and put the car in park. We sat there for a moment, neither of us saying anything, our minds both on other things. After a moment or so, we turned in our seats and start talking at the same time.

Laughing, I gestured, "You go first."

Sighing with anguish, Sid raked a hand through his hair, "I hate to say this, but I think tonight is a bust."

"Really? I was just going to say the same thing," I reached over and wrapped Sid's hand in mine, "I want to go on a date with you but maybe right now, with all that is going on it might have to wait a bit. Would that be okay?"

With a grim expression, Sid nodded, "As much as I'd like to pretend to be a normal human being, it's just not true. With my father on the loose, and that guy staying with you, romance might just have to wait."

"Romance, huh?" I couldn't help but tease, "Is that what this is?"

Sid gave a small chuckle, "Well, it was supposed to be. I know you don't have much thought on the whole sex without commitment thing, but most people do.

Especially women in this world." He frowned as though he'd remembered something bad, but then continued. "Normally, sex without the dating part would be fine with me but with you…it's different."

"Sidney," I said as I slid over to his side of the truck. I place my hands on either side of his face, "We haven't had sex yet."

This only made him frown harder, "Right. But still, I feel like we should be doing something. Exchange numbers, go on a date. You know, couple stuff."

I grinned at him. "I have your number, and while most people wouldn't call a car ride a date, we've hung out plenty of times outside of the bar. And if killing bad guys together doesn't constitute as couple stuff, then I don't know what does."

Sid's eyes softened before he drew my face up to his. Our mouths molded together briefly and a special tingly feeling started in my stomach causing Sid to pull back. His breathing heavy, he pressed his forehead to mine.

"Come on, let's get you back to your car before we give Peggy's a dinner show they won't soon forget."

Chuckling, I moved back to my side of the car as Sid pulled out of the parking lot. Normal might be something Sid wished for, but it was never something in my cards. Besides, how normal could a former archangel be?

4

AFTER SID DROPPED ME off at my car my cell phone rang. I glanced at the unknown number and frowned. I didn't make a habit of answering numbers I didn't know, but then again not many people had this number; all of my clients called the office.

"Mary Wiles," I answered as I started Trisha's car up.

There was a crackle and then a clearing of the throat before a vaguely familiar voice said, "I need you down at the precinct. Have a case for you."

The connection was bad enough it was hard to make out what the caller had even said, but only Thompson would call me without introduction and expect me to come running. Since my date had been a bust, as Sid had said, I had nothing better to do.

"I can be there in fifteen." I answered before ending the call. Thompson never waited for me to say goodbye so I didn't see the reason to do so either.

Pulling out of Gianni's, the smell of the food wafted in the air making my stomach growl. Two restaurant parking lots and no food. My body was not a happy camper. Guess it would be more like twenty minutes if I took the time to drive through somewhere.

Oh well, Thompson could wait. My stomach couldn't.

Thirty minutes and a bag of greasy burgers and fries later, I pulled into the West L.A. precinct parking lot. The line at the fast food place I'd stopped at had been longer than I'd anticipated, but the wait had been worth it. My stomach was happy and I was ready to face whatever Thompson had for me.

Stepping into the police station, I let the sounds of the office fill me. Everyone buzzed around like busy bees, all of them in such a hurry to save the world, or in the criminals—currently in the waiting rooms—to destroy it.

In general, I tried to avoid coming here. Most of the arrested were possessed by demons, which meant they automatically didn't like me. It made my walk through the open area to Thompson's office was filled with myriad taunts and snarls.

"Nasty bitch."

"Feathered whore."

"He's looking for you." The last one coming from a middle-aged woman struggling against her binds. On the street, she would look like a normal person. Dressed in gray slacks and a pale pink blouse she could even pass for a soccer mom, but with the veil dropped I could see what lay on the inside.

Swirling darkness and a molten red lining told me whoever this woman had been before was long gone. The only thing in there now was pure evil.

I took a cautious step toward her, keeping a good distance. My hand reached to touch my gun but then I remembered I had left it in the glove compartment, not expecting to need it on my date with Sid. Now, I was wishing I had it on me.

"Who's looking for me?" I asked, though I was pretty sure of the answer. There was only one person looking for me. One demon—who as Sid had said—wanted me to give him his powers back.

Instead of answering my question, the demon laughed, "You know who I speak of. The master is not patient."

I scoffed, "Well, he'll just have to wait, now won't he?"

The woman threw her head back and let out a sound I guessed was supposed to be a laugh, but it was more of a hiss. "Our master is not known for his patience, but you know that, don't you, fallen one?"

Before I could even think it, my hand was around her neck, lifting her and the chair she was handcuffed into the air. My teeth gnashed together as I growled, "I am not fallen!"

She didn't struggle as my hand squeezed around her throat; she let out a choking laugh. Hands grabbed at me but I shrugged them off. I vaguely heard the voices of officers shouting, but it wasn't until Thompson was by my side did I comprehend what was being said.

"Mary," Thompson's hand touched the arm holding the woman. He didn't yell it like the others. It was the calm tone that pulled my attention. I glanced away from the woman long enough to meet Thompson's eyes.

There was a strange emotion there. One I had never seen on his face.

Fear.

It shocked me enough that it made my anger wilt, and my grip on the woman loosened. The officers near us grabbed her from me, and as they dragged her away still chained to the chair, she laughed.

It was a good thing I didn't have my gun or I'd have shot her right there. Police station or no.

Once the woman was out of the room, Thompson latched onto my arm and I let him lead me into his office. The irrational anger I'd had experienced before had all but gone, leaving behind only a feeling of foolishness.

"What the hell has gotten into you?" Thompson roared once the door was closed. At his towering height, his rage would have instilled fear in even the lesser of men. But many of his officers, myself included, were used to it so the affect was lost on me.

"I don't know," I sighed, sitting in the chair in front of his desk. I placed my head in my hands and tried to figure out what had gotten into me.

"Mary." This time Thompson's voice was softer; the same as it had been back in the other room. His boots hit the ground as he moved toward me. The desk next to me creaked, letting me know he had sat beside me.

Staring hard at the ground, I said, "You have a lot of demons in your waiting area."

"Really?" the surprise in his voice caused it to rise an octave, "and the one you just assaulted in the middle of my precinct was —"

"A demon, yes." I cut him off, looking up from the ground.

"Hmmm," Thompson stared at the door in thought, "And that one what? Insulted your mother?" he said lightheartedly.

"Something like that."

"I have to say Wiles, I've never seen you like that," he gestured to the other room, "You lifted her clear off the ground without a sweat. Have you always been this strong?"

"Yes." I stared at him not elaborating further.

"You know, Wiles," Thompson shifted on top of the desk causing it to creak again, "I've never asked how you know so much about demons and such. Did you study it in school?"

I quirked a brow at him. After all this time, now he was asking?

Deciding to humor him, I said, "It's a family trait."

"It wouldn't happen to be a demonic trait, would it?" Thompson asked, tension in his posture as though asking the question was going to make me show my true face or something.

I laughed making Thompson jump in his seat, which only made me laugh harder. "No, Thompson, not a demonic trait. Think higher up."

At my admission Thompson's brows rose until they almost disappeared into his hair line. I didn't know why I was telling him this, in practice it wasn't good to let humans know about other beings; humans tended to jump the gun a bit, literally.

After a moment, Thompson nodded, "I could see that. And Trisha?"

"Is as human as they come."

"Good," he stood from the desk and moved around to the other side taking his seat, "So, besides your little disturbance what brings you down here?"

I frowned at his question, "What do you mean? You called me asking me to come. Said you had some case for me."

Thompson stared at me for a moment and then said, "No, I didn't. I've been up to my ears in the Billings case. Christy Fontanelle is a viper and is tearing our evidence to shreds. I don't have time to play with ghosts or demons."

My frown deepened. If it hadn't been Thompson on the phone then who? The only likely answer was Asmodeus; playing games and making me come down to the police station was his way of getting me in one spot. But then again, it was too public to have a showdown. Not unless he wanted to expose demons to the world.

But if not him, then who?

"Alright. Well, if you don't need me then I'm going to head home." I stood from my chair and headed for the door.

"Wiles?" I stopped at Thompson's voice and turned.

"What's heaven like?"

The question surprised me and I almost gave him a serious answer, but thought better of it. I shot him a smirk instead. "I wouldn't know."

As I made my way through the precinct the eyes of the officers' followed my every move. If I didn't know any better I'd say they were afraid of me. Couldn't be loved by everyone.

I kept my eyes forward though and resisted the urge. I had enough problems without making the whole West Side police force hate me. Plus, officers talk. If one part of the police force didn't like me, then the whole city would know about it and why.

It had gotten dark while I had been making a fool of myself. Enough so I really should have been wary of my surroundings. As it was, I was just ready to go home.

It wasn't until the sharp pain in the back of my head caused stars in my eyes before I realized what a mistake I'd made.

5

I SHOULD HAVE KNOWN better. First, the static-filled call and then Thompson not knowing what I'd been talking about. It should have all alerted me to be more careful. Instead I got clipped from behind.

Ramiel would be so disappointed in me.

The thought of my former commander forced me assess my situation. I tried to move my legs and arms, but they were bound snugly to the chair behind me. At least I was sitting up; it opened a whole new set of options lying down wouldn't have given me.

I tried not to move too much so as not to alert anyone of my consciousness. Keeping my eyes closed, I listened, but only the buzzing sound of electricity filled my ears.

Satisfied I was alone, I opened my eyes a crack. The lightening in the room wasn't very bright, as if someone had dimmed them for this very purpose. Opening my eyes wider, I scanned the space.

I could make out metal stands laid out with medical equipment. In front of me was an examination table, and to the side was a closed door.

I must be in some a hospital or clinic. But why would I be here? It didn't seem the kind of place Asmodeus would hole up in.

As if answering my question, the door to the room opened and revealed Doctor Ryan. Anger flared in me at seeing the short balding man.

He'd once patched me up after my first run-in with Asmodeus who thought I would look better with a blade through my stomach. Doctor Ryan could never let over how I had healed so quickly. Ever since, he'd been constantly badgering me to let him do some blood tests. I'd of course told him no, but he didn't seem to know the meaning of the word.

"Miss Wiles, you're awake. Good." He flicked the light switch causing the room to brighten and my eyes to squint.

"What the hell am I doing here?" I bit out, the fury in me only being kept at bay by reminding myself he was human.

Doctor Ryan looked at me as though my question was stupid. Then he held his hands out to the sides, "Well you are a medical miracle, Miss Wiles, and the world needs people like you."

"I already told you I wouldn't help you," I snapped, "This is illegal."

He cocked his head to the side and gave me a sly smile. "Now, now. You are one to talk about illegal."

I stared at him.

"Since you left the hospital, I've been watching you, Miss Wiles. You have quite the day job, almost more interesting than my own and definitely more dangerous. Some even illegal." He adjusted his glasses on the brim of his nose as he made his way around the room.

"Then, you know what kind of person I am," I warned, hoping it would be enough to make him hesitate. Sadly, it wasn't.

"Oh, yes," he chuckled, crossing his hands in front of him, "I have quite an idea of what kind of thing you are." The way he said thing it was as if I was something stuck on the bottom of his shoes. It didn't sit well for my situation. If he didn't consider me a human, then I was big trouble. Which meant I would have to hurt him. Something my angelic side loathed to do, but the side who had been aching to punch the smirking bastard in the face was more than ready for.

"So, what, you're going to keep me here and experiment on me?" I asked, adding a bit of a shiver shake to my voice so it would seem like he had me scared and helpless.

"Oh no, Miss Wile," He shook his head tucking, his hands into his lab coat, "While dissecting you would no doubt prove educational, I'm a doctor. My job is to heal the sick, and I believe your blood, your healing abilities could benefit mankind greatly."

"You know what I am, don't you, Doctor Ryan?" I asked straight out.

Ryan's mouth curved up into a smile, "I believe you are what most religions would call an angelic being."

"Then you know I'm not human. What makes you think my blood would be compatible with yours?" I watched him closely to see if my words were sinking in. "How do you know it won't kill some poor soul?"

"I don't," he shook his head as he picked a syringe off the metal stand, "But all experimental drugs come with their side-effects and risks. Yours is just one more."

He sat on rolling stool next to me and wrapped an elasticated strap around my upper arm. I watched as he felt around at the inside of my elbow for my vein.

Just before he slid the needle home he said, with quite a bit of confidence, "Besides, if God made us in his image, then you must be of the same cloth. And that makes us compatible."

The sting of the needle barely registered as I tried to find a way to make him understand. I didn't really know for sure what would happen if he put my blood in someone else, but I didn't think anything good would come of it. Maybe he would just have to learn the hard way.

"Are you going to bleed me dry and then dump me somewhere?" I asked after he filled the third vial.

"No, no," he tisked before popping the next tube in, "Who knows when someone like you will show up again? If I killed you before we've even begun to find out the extent of your healing abilities, then you couldn't help anyone."

"Then I'm to be your captive?"

Dr. Ryan lined up the vials in a little carrier and took them over to a mini fridge under the counter. "If I could trust you to return of your own volition then I'd be happy to let you walk out this door, but as it stands, I don't think I will be able to capture you a second time."

Damn straight he wouldn't. He'd be lucky if I didn't report him to the police for kidnapping. When I said as much he just smiled at me.

"And what would the police say to the evidence I have on your unusual activities?"

"You're bluffing." I shot back without hesitation. Even if he had anything on me, Thompson was on my side and now knew what I was, or at least had a suspicion.

"Not when it comes to the good of mankind," Dr. Ryan pressed his lips tightly together, "Now, I'm headed home for the evening, but I'll back in the morning. Do you need anything? A drink? Maybe I could insert a catheter?" he rubbed his chin thoughtfully.

"Touch me and die," I snapped.

His eyes narrowed and he dropped his hand. "Very well. I'll see you in the morning, Miss Wiles. We will do great things together, I just know it."

As soon as the door closed behind him, I struggled against the binds holding me to the chair. If that arrogant asshole thought I was just going to sit here like a good patient, then he had another thing coming.

The good doctor might have displaced the meaning of good, but he could tie a knot. I wouldn't just be able to rip through these like I had done when I had been captured by Asmodeus and his crew. I stopped struggling and closed my eyes. Breathing in and then out, I reached deep inside of myself. Some people would call it magic, but to me it was a part of myself; a holy aura which made up my entire being and was what allowed me to displace demons.

It surged up inside of me until it filled the very veins Dr. Ryan had been poking at. I flexed against the binds, and nothing. It still wasn't enough.

"Fuck!" I growled out and slumped in the chair. Either Doctor Ryan's blood draw had weakened me more than I'd expected, or the part of me that had been slowly becoming more human had decided to rear its ugly head.

Instead, of focusing on the inevitable end of my angelic existence, I searched the room for something to cut the ties with. Something glinted in the light and my eyes landed on the scalpel on the metal stand Dr. Ryan hadn't even bothered to move away from me.

Trying not to think about why he'd had a scalpel in here in the first place, I shifted my body weight, rocking to edge the chair closer. The legs scraped against the floor making me wince and pause. When no one came running, I continued my slow trek to the stand.

When I was close enough, I twisted so the fingers of my right reached out to drag the stand closer. My fingertips touched the edge of the scalpel and I leaned closer to try and grab it, only to have the chair topple over tossing both myself and the stand into the floor.

Wincing as my shoulder hit the ground, I smiled down at the scalpel in my hand. Flipping it over carefully, I worked on the ropes holding me in place. When the first one snapped, I quickly worked on the next before sitting up to do my legs.

Rubbing my wrists, I moved from the ground to my feet. I searched myself for my phone and realized with a groan that I'd left it in the car along with my gun. I did find my car keys, but it wouldn't help any if I was across town from the police station.

Sighing, I twisted the door handle and found it unlocked. Seriously? Was Dr. Ryan really this confident? Or just stupid?

I was betting on stupid.

Making my way through the doorway, my eyes peeled for the doctor I realized I was inside the hospital. An unused section, but the hospital no less. Which meant I could find a phone. I'd need one since my car was currently way further than I cared to walk to.

I found the elevator and pressed the button for the lobby. Luckily, it wasn't a busy time of day, or rather night, because I went straight to the ground floor without stopping. I walked out of the elevator and right into Adara.

"Mary!" Adara cried her dark eyes widening. "What are you doing here?"

After realizing who I had assaulted, I performed an uncharacteristic move and hugged her.

"Um, not that I don't appreciate the extra lovin', but do you want to tell me what's going on?"

Letting her go, I stepped back. "You have no idea how happy I am to see you. Do you have a car?"

"Yes?" she nodded her brows raising.

"Then, you can give me a ride back to mine and I'll tell you all about it." I wrapped an arm around her shoulders and led the ex-demon hunter toward the exit.

6

DURING THE RIDE TO my car, I explained what happened to Adara. The weird phone call, arriving at the police station, Thompson not knowing what I was talking about, and then get smacked on the back of the head, only to wake up to have Dr. Ryan draw blood from me.

"I hope he doesn't put it in anyone," Adara commented after I was done, "There's no telling what could happen. If God wanted angels and humans to be together, then he would have made it that way."

"Exactly," I agreed, "It's stupid to think Ryan won't try to use it." I remembered his eyes, filled with eagerness to do something good for humanity. While, his intentions were good, his method of execution had already put him down the path of damnation.

"What are you going to do if he does?" Adara looked at me briefly before turning her eyes back to the road.

I shrugged, "I don't know. I'll deal with it when it comes to it. I don't know for certain anything bad will happen but I can say nothing good will come of it."

We were quiet for the rest of the ride. Adara's face was pinched in thought. She was more worried about Ryan than I was, but then again, she used to be one of those people whose main purpose in life was to protect humans.

Just because she wasn't part of the demon-hunter guild she was raised in anymore didn't mean she didn't still have the same conviction to do good. I couldn't say the same. An angel, yes, but a saint? Not even close. If Ryan hurt someone because of his inability to accept the word 'no', then it was his problem not mine. I was in the business of killing demons, not dealing with humans.

At least, I used to be.

We pulled into the West L.A. precinct and as Adara parked the car she turned to me. Uh oh. She had that look in her eye. The one she got when she was going to lecture me about my unfeeling ways.

"Look, I'm not trying to tell you what to do," she started.

"But?" I raised a brow at her.

"But, you really shouldn't just brush your encounter with Doctor Ryan off."

"Why not? He's not going to get the drop on me again, and if he knows what's good for him he'll keep his distance." Though, the likelihood of that happening wasn't high.

"Just hear me out. What if something bad doesn't happen? What if what he'd hoped would happen does? Then he tells people and you end up on the world's most wanted list. Then what? Are you just going to shoot them all?"

"If I must," I said dryly.

"Seriously, Mary," Adara eyes narrowed on me, "You need to get your blood back before he can use it on anyone. If you don't want to do it then I can get someone from the guild to do it."

I let out a groan and tugged at my hair. "Fine. Have one of your guys do it. That way, if he's already figured out I'm gone, he can't try to trap me again."

Adara pulled her cell phone out and pressed a button before putting the phone to her ear. "Hey Burges, yeah it's me. I need a favor. Yeah, off the books."

I sat there as she explained the situation to the Burges person on the other end of the line. After a few moments, she turned to me and asked, "Where's the blood now?"

Thinking back to the examination room, I said, "It's in a mini fridge in the room I was kept in."

"And where was that?" Adara's tone a bit impatient.

"I don't know," I shrugged, "I came out of the room and went straight for the elevators. I didn't stop to read all the signs," I explained and then paused, "But it wasn't a floor in use. The lights were out—except for the security ones—and there weren't any other patients or employees I could see."

"Did you get all that Burges?" Burges' voice echoed loudly on the other end of the line and Adara barked back, "Then check every one of them. We can't let this blood get into the wrong hands."

Rapid unintelligible words burst from Adara's phone. Adara appeared unaffected and ended the call with, "Alright, fine. Let me know when you have it."

When she hung up, she looked up at me. "One problem taken care of."

"Thanks," I offered her a grin and a nod.

"No problem," she shoved me on the shoulder returning my grin, "What are friends for?" Adara paused and then her grin wilted slightly. "Speaking of friends. How's Ramiel doing?"

This was the second person today to ask me about my former commander. I didn't know why I was irritated about it; it was only natural they would want to inquire about the guy I had been looking for the last five years. Though, I had a feeling Sid's inquires had more to do with jealousy than curiosity.

"He's as well as he can be expected," I answered stiffly.

"Still not talking?"

I'd only told two people my suspicions about Ramiel's descent from heaven. One being Trisha and the other Adara. As an ex-demon hunter with a penchant for getting in bed with the enemy, I knew she wouldn't judge me for keeping Ramiel around to get information.

"No, he's not. But he will soon."

"How do you know?" she quirked a brow, "Did Madame Serena read your fortune? Or have you developed your own psychic skills now?"

"No," my response was clipped, "But I do know Ramiel—or at least I did—and after today he will be well on his way to trying to pacify me."

"And what about Sid? What does he think of all of this?" She didn't need to spell out what she meant. Adara didn't agree with me keeping Sid in the dark about Ramiel's position. She believed the secret wasn't good for our budding relationship—or my safety.

Usually, I took her advice to heart, but not this time. I wanted to keep the knowledge of Ramiel's falling limited to as few people as possible. Even if I thought Sid would blow a gasket, I also didn't know how well his father was tracking him. If Ramiel was working with Asmodeus, I didn't want him to know I was on to him just yet.

"He thinks I should be careful. As he should," I ignored the way Adara's eyes narrowed and continued, "He also thinks

Asmodeus is going to come after me and the dagger."

"Which is safe, I hope?" Adara stopped glaring at me long enough to look worried.

"Of course," I reached down and pulled my left pant leg up, exposing the sheath strapped to my calf. Ever since the events at the hotel, when I was supposed to trade the dagger for Ramiel's life, I'd kept the dagger close to me, never letting it out of my sight and never leaving Ramiel alone with it.

"But," I sighed, unsnapping the dagger from my leg and holding it out to Adara, "I think you should take it back to the guild for safe-keeping." Adara reached out to take it but I jerked it back, "And not in some display case where anyone could steal it the way I did. I mean, in some dank dark dungeon where only the one who put it there will ever be able to find it."

Adara nodded and I slowly handed over the dagger. It felt wrong somehow, parting with it. It was meant for someone like me; an archangel.

It had been Michael's at one point, until he had been too arrogant and had lost it during the dark ages. The dagger was one of the only ways to create a portal between hell and earth. Only a really powerful witch, or high-level demon, could open one. Even then there were rules in place which kept the process from being so easy.

"What are you going to do now?" Adara asked, clipping the sheath to her own calf, "I can't keep it hidden forever. Eventually, someone will find it."

"I know," I stared out the front window of the car, letting the light from the precinct make my eyes blur., "I have to find some way to destroy it—or get it off this plane—and at the same time keep Asmodeus off my back and away from my loved ones."

Adara laughed. "A tall order but if anyone can do it, you can."

"Thanks." I smirked, wishing I had as much confidence in myself as she did in me.

I opened the door to her car and put one foot out, then stopped. Turning slightly in the seat, I glanced back at her. "I forgot to ask how you were. How's the bar scene?"

Something flashed across Adara's face—an emotion I couldn't place—but she covered it up with a mischievous grin. "Oh, you know, same old drink to pour, same old demons to bed."

"Don't you get tired of it?" I asked, watching her closely. Something was up with my friend, but if I knew Adara she wouldn't let on what it was until she was good and ready to.

Surprisingly, she admitted, "Sometimes I miss the action, the day-to day-danger and turmoil. But then that's what I have you for, now don't I?" Adara placed her hand on my shoulder.

"Of course," I responded, placing my hand on top of hers, "but if you change your mind, let me know. I could always use another assistant."

"Hey!" Adara shouted as I stepped of the car and into the night. I chuckled to myself as I made my way to Trisha's car.

Adara and I would make one kick-ass demon-hunting machine, I had no doubt. But the demons Adara really needed to fight were her own, and until then she was better off keeping on the sidelines. I just prayed she'd stay that way.

7

I HADN'T PAID MUCH attention to the time until I got home and Madame Serena's glowing sign was off. I glanced up to the windows above her shop, where my office sat, and frowned at the lights blazing from all the windows.

Trisha should have gone home by now.

I opened the glove compartment and grabbed my gun—a Glock 42 which Adara had given me when we first met. I used to be skittish about using it, too afraid of hurting some innocent bystander in the process, but with more and more demons showing their ugly faces, it was faster to put a holy bullet through their head than to try and exorcise each of them one by one.

Keeping the gun in my hand, I took slow precise steps out of the car and up the stairs. I made sure to skip over the third riser from the top; lately it had had a tendency to squeak—which reminded me to ask Madame Serena about fixing it. Good for knowing when company was coming, bad for trying to get the jump on your enemies.

I paused briefly outside the office door before reaching out and twisting the door handle. Locked. Maybe Trisha had gone home after all? I pulled out my keys, but before I could put them in the slot the door yanked open and Trisha screamed.

"Mary! Where the hell have you been?" Normally, Trisha would have an attitude in her question, but this time it seemed more panicked than anything.

"Long story, I'll explain later," I followed her back inside and immediately noticed my office door was open. Without a word, I walked into the office and searched for Ramiel.

"He left a while ago," Trisha explained coming up behind me, "I tried to call you, but there was no answer. At first, I figured you and Sid were getting it on, but then when one hour become two, I started to get a little panicky.”

“Sorry. I left my phone in the car with my gun,” I gave her an apologetic look, “And Sid and I didn’t even get to the date portion of the night before we had to call it quits.”

“Quits?” Trisha exclaimed, “as in kaput, no more Sidary?”

“Sidary?” I cocked a brow at her, “No, not like that. His powers have been out of whack ever since his father came through. We almost did it in the parking lot.”

“Oh,” Trisha drew out, “Well, that’s good at least.” She shrugged, then stopped and pointed at me, “But if you weren’t with Sid, where were you? I tried the sergeant but he said you’d left about twenty minutes before I’d called.”

“Well, that’s where it gets interesting.” I explained to her about Doctor Ryan and then filled her in on the situation with Adara. When I was finished Trisha looked more stressed out than when she had when I had arrived.

"Do you think we can really find a way to get rid of the dagger?" she asked chewing on the nail of her thumb.

"I don't know," I admitted, staring down at the blade in thought.

"There has to be some way to destroy it, or give it back. I mean, it can't be completely indestructible, can it?" Trisha moved across the room and sat down at my desk. She turned the computer on and started to type on the keyboard, an intense focus in her eyes. "I can search the net but it might take a while to find something on the dagger's powers. The first time we looked for it there wasn't much to be found."

I sat on the edge of the desk opposite of her, "Well, do what you can but not tonight. It's been a long night for both of us, and we will do better in the morning after some sleep."

Frowning, Trisha nodded, "Alright. Mom's probably going to flip on me anyways for being out so late. She's still spitting venom about her last visit."

While Trisha might look like an undead groupie, she had a softer heart than anyone I knew. Her mother on the other hand, was a hard-as-nails stepford wife who thought I was the bad influence. An archangel a bad influence? Who knew?

Trisha gathered her things and made for the door. Before she left though, she asked, "What about Ramiel? Are you going to go look for him?"

I shook my head, "No. If he left it would have been for a reason. I'm sure he will be back on his own. After all, where else would he go?"

Trisha nodded, but I could see the uncertainty in the movement. I didn't want to worry her more by adding on what I was really thinking.

Where else would Ramiel go? The phone call I had walked in on earlier came back to mind and put even more doubt in my mind. He was hiding something, something else other than his fallen status. I just hoped it wasn't what I suspected it to be. I needed more people in my corner and less in the Asmodeus's.

* * *

THAT NIGHT, I SLEPT better than I had since Ramiel had come to stay with me. Probably because I wasn't constantly fighting the need to vomit from his close proximity.

When I woke it was just after eight and Trisha could already be heard clacking away at the keys in the reception area. Frowning, I wondered why she hadn't awakened me. She usually couldn't wait to disturb my sleep with her strange questions.

Slipping out of bed, I grabbed my gun out of the bed holster and held it low by my side. Ramiel still hadn't returned; his side of the bed was unslept in and there was no sight of him. I crept across the room and slowly opened the office door. Jumping out into the room, I pointed the barrel of the gun toward where Trisha's desk was and let out a heavy breath.

Trisha sat behind the computer, her eyes focused solely on the monitor in front of her. She hadn't even looked up when I had almost shot her. As I made my way over to her, I took in her haggard appearance.

The colorful extension in hair were gone, and her dark hair was piled on her head in a messy bun. She wore a baggy t-shirt with a logo on it—one I didn't recognize. It could have been from any number of things she was into. For a moment, I thought I might be dreaming because she was wearing jeans. Plain old, blue jeans with not a tear in or safety pin in sight.

She must really be worried.

"Did you find anything?" I asked putting my gun on the table before going over to the coffee pot we kept for visitors. Trisha usually started a pot right when she got there, caffeine being her drug of choice, but it was empty. I tried to keep away from stimulant; alcohol and caffeine didn't set well with my angelic make up, making me either hallucinate or jitter out of my skin. Today though, I could have really used a cup.

I started a pot while Trisha kept typing. The sound of the brewer going finally pulled her out of her concentration because she shot her eyes to me briefly to say, "Pour me a cup will ya?"

"Sure." I grabbed one of our two coffee cups and filled it three fourths of the way full before adding creamer. I might not drink the stuff but I still remembered how my assistant drank it.

"I've been up most of the night trying to find some way to destroy that damned dagger but nothing." Trisha growled and tossed her pen down.

"You didn't have to do that. I told you to get some sleep, not take your work home with you," I chastised sitting on the edge of her desk.

Trisha sighed and dragged her hands over the sides of her face, "I know, but if we get rid of the dagger then Asmodeus has no other reason to come after us, right?"

Giving the liquid one final stir, I handed the cup over. "You mean besides the fact that I'm the only one who can take the charm off?"

"Ugh, I forgot about that," Trisha made a face before taking a drink of her coffee, "and thank you caffeine."

"Anyways, if you can't find a way to destroy it then our only other option is to contact an angel to take it back to heaven." I crossed my arms over my chest and stared across the room.

"Can you do that?" Trisha looked up from her coffee long enough to ask.

Yes. No. It was a hard question. One which didn't have a simple answer. I'd tried before to contact someone from heaven to try and find a way back home without my wings, but it had never worked before.

The jiggle of bells signaled the opening of Madame Serena's shop and an idea began to form. I grabbed my gun off the table where I had sat it and found my spare holster in Trisha's desk drawer.

"Where are you going?" Trisha asked without even looking up from her computer.

Heading for the door, I said, "To see if I can place a celestial call."

8

A BELL DINGED AS I opened the door to Madame Serena's shop. Incense filled my nose making me sneeze.

"Hello?" Madame Serena's voice called out from further in the store. "You'll have to forgive me, I'm not quite ready for customers yet."

"Then shouldn't you keep your sign off?" I teased.

"Mary? Is that you?"

"You're the psychic. You tell me," I replied, wondering why I felt the need to be so contrary today.

Madame Serena snorted, "Give me a moment and I'll be right there." There was crash followed by a few mumbled curses.

Chuckling, I said, "No worries. Take your time."

While I waited for my landlord to come out, I scanned the shop. I'd only been in here a few times. Usually, when I couldn't get a hold of her on the phone. I hadn't paid much attention then, but I was now.

Glass display cases lined one side of the shop, filled with all sorts of mythical like charms and crystals. There was even one which looked like the charm I'd put around Asmodeus's neck. It made me wonder if the parts even mattered, or if only the power behind the creation made all the difference.

I moved on from the glass cases and strolled over to a shelf in the front corner.

Bottles of all shapes and sizes sat on the wooden shelf. Some of them were colored and others glowed an unearthly glow. I picked up a glowing lime-green bottle and lifted it to eye level.

The liquid inside swirled and churned as if pushed by some inner force. I pulled the stopper out and gave it a sniff. Jerking back at the pungent scent, I quickly sealed it again.

I placed the bottle back on the shelf and turned, "You know, I've never really looked around your shop before. You have some interesting stuff here."

"Bah, touristy trash," Madame Serena's scoffed as she came out of a door behind the glass counter. She waved a hand at the shelf holding the glowing bottles. "I add a bit of real magic to keep their interest, but most of it is colored water and herbs."

Crossing my arms over my chest I nodded. Most people would call it illegal, but what Madame Serena did was her own business. Besides, if she kicked me out I highly doubted I'd find a better place. I already suspected Adara had had a hand in getting me my office-slash-home. I was sure if anyone really took the time they could figure out my whole life was fabricated.

Then I'd be in more than a little trouble. So, if my landlady wanted to sell stinky water to some tourists, who was I to point fingers?

Madame Serena's eyes locked onto me, pupils almost disappearing into the dark color of her irises. "Now, I know you didn't come down here to chit chat about my shop. You're not the type. What do you need?"

I walked over to a table she had set up for readings and leaned against the edge. "I was hoping you'd be able to help me get in contact with an angel."

"An angel?" Madame Serena's brows rose in surprise, "What do you need me for? You're an angel, can't you call your own kind?"

I shook my head and frowned, "You know it doesn't work like that. Besides, I've tried before and either they aren't listening or they're ignoring me."

The bangles she wore on her arms clanged as she walked over to me. "Why would they do that? You're one of them. It's not like you chose to stay here."

"Doesn't matter. I'm as good as fallen to them." I didn't try to hide bitterness in my voice. I wasn't a hundred percent sure if I actually got in contact with another angel I wouldn't go a bit crazy on them for leaving me on earth to fend for myself.

Sitting down at the table, Madame Serena pulled out a candle and a few crystals. "Alright, I won't pretend to know the inner workings of the divine, so I'll just take your word for it." She gestured for me to take a seat across from her and then asked, "So who should we call, and what do you want to say?"

That was a good question. Since it was Michael's blade it stood to reason I should call him to take it back. But the thought of dealing with the arrogant Hand of God did not appeal to me.

If Ramiel wasn't currently on earth already, he'd be the first person I'd have called. If he was MIA and on my possible enemy list I'd have asked his advice on who to contact but thinking about it, there really was only one other angel I could think of to help me.

"I want to call on Uriel. She's one of the only ones who might be open to helping me." Not that she had come when I had called before, I added internally.

Madame Serena gave me a questioning look but didn't comment. "Alright, let's get started," she held her hands out across the table, but when I simply stared at them she sighed, "We have to touch to make a connection. It's like a telephone; I can't just dial a random number and get who I want. I need a bit of guidance."

"If you must." I placed my hands in hers and found them surprisingly rough.

Seeming to notice my surprise, Madame Serena said, "Don't look so surprised. I lived on a farm the first half of my life. I wasn't always at the guild's beck-and-call." The way she said it told me she didn't exactly like her part in all this.

I didn't ask and she didn't offer up the details instead, she gripped my hands

94

lightly and closed her eyes. She muttered a few words and a gust of wind blew lightly through the shop. The wind chimes, which lined the window of shop, bumped against each other providing a soft background noise.

"Concentrate, Mary," Madame Serena's chastised me as I looked around us, "You need to be thinking about who you want to contact. Envision them answering your call."

I forced back the urge to snort. The whole think-it-and-it-will-be mentality had never been something I believed in. I did believe Uriel would answer the call if she wouldn't get in trouble for it. She was worse than I was about following the rules.

I smiled to myself as I thought about what she would think of me now. A rebel no doubt. She might even go so far as to say I was as bad as a fallen. Though, my goals were far more righteous than any of them. For a moment, I wondered what Ramiel's goals might be.

"Probably the same as all the rest," a bell-like voice answered the question I hadn't asked out loud.

My head jerked up in the direction of the new voice. Cloaked in a floor-length dress of white lace, Uriel's blue eyes exuded her disapproval. Her wings—the color of new snow—curled down behind her as holy presence threatened to overtake us.

Frozen in her seat, I couldn't expect Madame Serena to be of any help. I turned back to the angel and scowled, "You know, it's rude to listen in on another's thoughts."

"So is calling on an archangel for a social call." Uriel crossed her arms over her chest and settled a disapproving stare on me. Then after a moment, we both broke into a smile. I stood from my seat and embraced her, finding it strange to have to avoid her wings.

"Muriel," she breathed, releasing me from the hug, "I'm so sorry."

"I know," I shook my head, trying to stop her from explaining, "You have to think of yourself. I don't blame you for not coming sooner." It was true. I didn't blame her or any of the other angels. Who I did blame was the big guy, though. He's supposed to help his children, but so far, he hasn't done anything for me. It made me wonder why I even bothered trying to get home.

"You know that's not true," my eyes narrowed at Uriel and she put her hands up, "Sorry, sorry. I can't help it sometimes. But still, you know it doesn't work like that."

"Like what?" the question came from Madame Serena who had finally snapped out of her awe of Uriel.

Uriel turned her attention to the psychic. "God. He doesn't just help you just because you ask for it, and he also doesn't give you more than you can handle."

I sniffed and forced back the retort on the top of my tongue. Instead I said, "That's not what we called you for anyways."

"I know," Uriel replied and then lowered her head, "But I can't help you. I don't know anything about Michael's blade. You should have called Michael himself.”

“As if he would come?” I scoffed, “I'm lucky you even answered my call.”

“And I shouldn't be here. I'm taking a huge risk coming here.” Uriel pointed a finger at me.

“If you couldn't help, then why did you come?” Madame Serena asked, “Why take the risk?”

Uriel's gaze softened on me, “Because Muriel is one of my oldest friends and I hate how you've suffered so much on your own.” She shook her head sadly, her eyes glistening with unshed tears. Uriel had always been one of the few angels to feel emotions. Most of us barely registered those around us, let alone cared enough to make friends. Save Ramiel, I’d have included myself in that majority.

“I didn’t say I couldn’t help,” Uriel said primly, “It’s true I don’t know how to destroy it and I can’t take it back with me.”

"Why not?" Madame Serena asked, but before Uriel could answer I stepped in.

"You don't know what it's like there, Serena," Uriel and I exchanged a look of mutual understanding, "If Uriel took the dagger to heaven and started asking around, then someone would eventually want to know where she got it from."

"Which," Uriel jumped in, "in turn, would lead to how I got in contact with Muriel and then I could very well find myself fallen, like Ramiel."

The mention of Ramiel caused me to fall silent. Uriel's eyes widened and then turned to concern. She placed a hand on my arm and I forced myself not to flinch.

"You did know, didn't you?"

I let out a heavy sigh. "I suspected, but you just confirmed it."

"Oh, I'm sorry, Muriel. I thought you knew." Uriel shook her head solemn expression covering her face.

"No, I didn't," I replied, and then after a moment a thought came to me. "How long did you know?"

Cocking her head to the side, Uriel asked, "That Ramiel was fallen?" I nodded. "From the beginning, that's why no one went after him when it was reported he was taken by demons. He had already fallen at that point. We thought you knew and were choosing exile as well."

Anger flared within me. Gnashing my teeth, I grabbed her by the arms, "If I knew Ramiel was fallen do you really think I would have followed after him? I thought everyone was abandoning him. I thought I was saving him!"

Uriel winced and I loosened my grip on her arms. Taking in deep calming breaths, I turned my back on Uriel and Madame Serena's startled expressions. What exactly had they expected? My whole existence, all my suffering, had been for nothing. Sure, I'd suspected Ramiel was fallen but I hadn't really grasped what it meant to me. Now, I did and it didn't just make me mad. The fires of hell had nothing on the burning rage inside of me.

"I think I should go," Uriel said after a moment, "I'll ask around about destroying the dagger and how to get you your wings back."

"Thank you," I muttered but didn't turn around. My anger was slowly morphing to grief, and I could feel the tears prickling at my eyes.

Wind swooshed through the room and then she was gone. The bangles on Madame Serena's arm clinked as she stood from the table. She came up behind me and she placed a hand on my shoulder.

"Are you alright, Mary?"

I could hear the pity in her voice and I hated it. I shrugged off her hand and started for the door. "I'm fine. Thanks for your help."

"Mary," Madame Serena's voice stopped me at the door, "You might be an angel, but part of you is more human than celestial, and humans need others. You can't do this alone."

I opened the door without answering her, letting it slam shut behind me. Part of me knew what Madame Serena said was true, but the other half fought not to believe it. Pulling my phone out of my pocket, I dialed the first person I thought who would understand how I felt.

Sid.

9

SID DIDN'T ANSWER THE phone the first time I called him—nor the next dozen times I called over the next few days. Worry ate at me and I was just about ready to march down to the bar to give him a piece of my mind when Ramiel walked through the front door of my office.

"Well, look what the cat dragged in," Trisha commented from her desk. After her initial bad luck with the dagger search she had gone back to her usual full face of makeup and extravagant clothing. While, disappointed at her results, I was happy to see her back to her normal chipper, but slightly sarcastic, self.

Ramiel shot a look of disdain at Trisha, "I don't see what concern it is to you, human."

103

Trisha huffed, poking her bottom lip out in a pout. That was it. I'd had it.

"You might not think you have to report to Trisha, but it is my concern," I snapped coming toe-to-toe with my former commander. His eyes widened and then his expression changed to one I knew only too well.

It was that of the archangel Ramiel, High Commander of the Fifth Division of God's Holy Army. A look I hadn't seen since we'd rescued him from Asmodeus. The intensity in his face used to make legions of angels follow his every command, but it only served to piss me off further.

"How dare you—"

"No," I cut him off, "How dare you?" and then it like a dam being broken as it all spilled out, "I left heaven to save you. I was captured by demons and tortured, my wings cut off, for you!"

"But—" Ramiel tried to speak, but I shoved a finger at his chest.

"I'm still talking. You might have been a big shot in heaven, but this is my city. My office. You are going to listen to me. I thought I was saving you. I believed I was the only one who cared enough about you to take on the demons. But what do I find out?"

I paused for a moment turning to Trisha and then back to Ramiel. "Then I find out the person I thought I was saving didn't want to be saved!" I let out a harsh laugh, "What a fool I was to think the great Ramiel would be captured by demons. I should have known better than to think you would be taken anywhere you didn't want to be."

"I can explain," Ramiel finally got out.

"I'm sure you can," I growled, "But right now, I don't want to hear it. In fact, I don't want to look at you at all."

"Muriel."

"Mary. For the last time, my name is Mary," I practically shouted, "Now, get the hell out of my office." I pointed at the door and Ramiel's face fell. I almost felt bad for him, but then he had to go and open his mouth.

His bright blue eyes hardened, "This isn't over."

After he slammed the door behind him, I let out a heavy sigh. A slow clap started from behind me and I turned, offering Trisha a lopsided grin.

"Way to go Mary!" she hopped up from her seat and flounced across the room, "I was wondering how long you were going to let that asshole stay here."

I ran a hand through my hair and then placed it on Trisha's shoulder, "No one talks to my girl like that. He has overstayed his welcome."

I had filled Trisha in on what I'd learned from Uriel the moment I had gotten back. My assistant had been so outraged she'd wanted to hunt down Ramiel right then and kick his sorry ass—her words not mine. I told her he wasn't worth it and with how he just acted, I realized he really wasn't. I didn't understand how I had ever seen anything in him in the first place. But then again, I had been a different person in heaven. Now, I had a different set of standards, those which had found me someone even better. If he would only answer the damned phone.

"I'm going to go by Sid's and see what's going on," I explained to Trisha as I made my way to the door. When I opened it, something fell against my legs, making me jump back.

"Doctor Ryan?" I glared down at the semi-conscious doctor. He still wore his lab coat, except his glasses were missing and his skin had turned a deathly ashen color. I was half-tempted to kick his sorry butt back down the stairs, but for some reason unknown to me, I lifted him off the ground and brought him inside. I practically dumped him on the couch causing him to let out an oomph.

"Mary!" Trisha cried out, rushing over to the doctor's side, "Can't you see he's sick."

"Yeah," I scowled, "Probably from my blood."

Doctor Ryan cracked open his eyes. When they landed on me, relief filled them, instilling shame in me. "Miss Wiles," Doctor Ryan's voice was weak, but somehow still sounded educated and refined, "Thank God."

I stood as his side while Trisha knelt by him, clutching his hand in hers. "What are you doing here?"

Trisha shot me a disapproving look before turning back to the Doctor.

"It's as you said," he said slowly, "I used your blood on myself this morning and then I started to feel sick. I didn't know where else to go. No one else would believe me. I should have listened to you when you told me no." He coughed, a wracking sound which lasted long enough for Trisha to jump up and get him a glass of water. She offered the water to the doctor as I paced in front of them.

"How did you even get my blood anyways?" I asked, "It should have been taken from you by now."

Doctor Ryan let out a small laugh which caused another coughing fit. "You are right. Your friends did come and the blood I had taken from you had all but been taken. But one."

My lips pressed into a thin line at his explanation. I'd have to let Adara know her Burges friend had failed. If I knew anything about Adara, she wouldn't be happy and there would be hell to pay.

"So," I crossed my arms over my chest, "You decided to continue with your tests, but instead of getting some poor victim to test it on you used it on yourself?" I arched a brow, "You weren't sick though."

Doctor Ryan swallowed some more water from the glass Trisha held to his mouth, and then croaked, "No, I wasn't. But I wanted to make sure it had no adverse effects on healthy humans before trying to give it to someone with an illness." When I only stared at him in disbelief he continued, "I don't expect you to believe me but I've studied your blood extensively. I saw nothing which could have caused such a reaction."

"No. You wouldn't," I murmured.

In a moment's thought, I dropped the veil and stared down at the doctor. His soul was whiter than I had expected, which made me think his intentions were purer than I had originally thought. I searched his body for what I suspected and found it in his left arm where he must have injected my blood into his body. There, swirling around lay a golden light. The light, barely visible, slithered out in almost vein-like strands.

It was as I had thought.

"What is it Mary?" Trisha asked, looking to me expectantly.

I sighed, weary from everything already. Still, I explained, "Some cultures believed when you donate a part of yourself, like an organ, or even blood, you are giving a part of yourself. Your essence goes into the person. I think," I gestured to the doctor, "Doctor Ryan took some of my essence into himself when he put my blood inside of his body."

Trisha glanced back down at the doctor, a frown marring her face. "So, is your essence killing him?"

Doctor Ryan glanced at Trisha and then to me. There must have been something on my face because he said, "I believe, what Miss Wiles is trying to say is I've been infected."

"Infected?" Trisha cried, shooting me a look. "But how? You're an angel shouldn't your blood heal." I gave her an incredulous frown and she hurried to add, "I mean I'm not agreeing with his methods but you can't blame me for going there. Anyone else would think so as well."

"No one listens to me," I threw my hands up, "I said I didn't know for sure what would happen but this isn't really so farfetched." I jerked an arm at Doctor Ryan, who looked sicker by the minute. I'd be proud of my strong genes if it wasn't killing him.

"Well, can't you do anything?" Trisha pleaded, the worry in her eyes sent a pang into my heart.

Damn her and her doe eyes. Though, I couldn't really leave him like this anyways. Not when he was right in front of me. If he had stayed away and died I might have been able to accept it, but now he was here. I had to try and save him.

I knelt by Trisha's side, thinking out loud, "I don't know for sure if I can do anything really but...if it's my essence hurting him, if I can remove it then it stands to reason he'll get better."

"You think so?" Trisha asked, a hopeful gleam in her eye.

I shrugged, "It's worth a shot. Besides, I can't hurt him any worse." I smiled slightly at Doctor Ryan, hoping to lighten the mood.

"Do what you can," he breathed out before coughing once more.

I waited for him to finish before dropping the veil once more. I reached into my pocket for the talisman. It was made by a gypsy—from one of my remaining feathers—to help focus my holy power in my physical form on earth. I used to use it all the time to exorcise demons, but since I had gotten my gun-shyness it's more of a keep sake. But the kind of focus I needed now couldn't come from a bullet. I just hoped it worked.

"Now, this shouldn't hurt...I don't think." My brow furrowed as I tried to concentrate. I figured it was kind of like exorcising a demon. When I force a demon out of the host's body I pour my aura into it. Now, I just had to do the reverse and prayed I didn't kill the good doctor in the process.

Wrapping the talisman around my hand, I pressed it against the entry point where my aura was the strongest. Usually, when the human was worth saving I slowly pushed my power into them. This time I had to take small pulls, like sipping from a straw. Working on it for a few minutes, I didn't think it was working because the doctor showed no change, but then the screaming started.

Doctor Ryan thrashed on the couch, almost dislodging me from my position. I held fast and kept at it. I could now see the golden light flowing in the opposite direction, and the faster it went the more he screamed.

"Stop it, Mary," Trisha yelled, trying to pull me away, "You're killing him."

I shrugged her off, "If I stop he will die. Now, quiet so I can concentrate."

I wished it would have been like pulling off a band aid, but I didn't know what it would do to Doctor Ryan if I tried to go faster. Instead, I had to move at a slow and torturous pace, which had the doctor screaming until he eventually passed out. It made the work quieter, but not any less strenuous. Eventually, though, I reabsorbed the last bit of golden energy back into myself.

I collapsed next to the couch, breathing heavily. Trisha sat down beside me, her worried expression making me smile weakly. "It's done. Whether or not it works, I don't know. We just have to wait and see."

"You did good, Mary," Trisha brushed aside the hair now matted against the side of my face.

I gave a short laugh. "Let's just hope it doesn't turn around to bite me in the ass."

10

"WILL HE BE OKAY?" Trisha asked me after I'd finally regained my strength.

Taking in the doctor's condition, I said with uncertainty, "I wish I could say for sure, but based on how his color is improving I'd say he's better than he was when he arrived." I dropped the veil and gave his soul a cursory glance. No golden color in sight.

"Hmm." Trisha's brow furrowed worry on her face. I didn't blame her. It wasn't often we had to worry about the lives of others in this way. With exorcisms either they were already dead or if they were lucky they'd survived the extraction of the demon. More often than not though, they didn't survive long. But those situations were very different than the one we were currently dealing with.

For some reason, I wished Sid was here. Though, he wasn't any more likely to know anything about Doctor Ryan's situation than I was, I just felt like he should be here. If only he would answer his damned phone.

Pulling my phone out of my pocket I glared at the screen as I hit Sid's number for the hundredth time. It rang twice before going to voicemail. Growling, I opened my mouth to leave a scathing message when the office door opened and Sid popped his head in.

"Anyone home?" he asked in a smooth voice, but now it did nothing to soothe my irritation. His dark hair fell over his eyes and I wondered—despite my annoyance—if his eyes had always been such a deep shade of emerald green.

Pushing the thought aside, I hung up the phone and stomped across the room. "Why haven't you answered your phone?"

Sid stepped inside and tucked his hands into his pockets as he always did when he was feeling insecure. I usually thought it was pretty adorable but at the moment it just irritated me more. "Geez, Mary, I'm sorry. I lost my phone a few days ago and haven't had a chance to get a new one." My frown deepened at his answer and Sid closed the distance between us. He took my hands in his, an unusual thing for him to do all of a sudden, but I forgot about it the instant his hands touched mine.

It suddenly became hard to breathe, as if all the air had been sucked out of the room. My chest lifted and fell in quick succession as I tried to regain my breath. Sid's thumb rubbed along my hand in a circular motion and each swipe of his finger felt as if it were touching things low within me. I ripped my hands from his and took a step back. Instantly, breathing became easier but my body still tingled where he had touched me.

"You haven't fed recently, have you?" I asked, moving further into the room where Trisha watched with increasing interest.

"I fed this morning actually." Sid shrugged as if it were no big deal. His mesmerizing gaze briefly moved from me to the doctor laying on the couch. "Who's he?"

My brow scrunched down at Sid's question. "It's Doctor Ryan. He took care of me after your dad stabbed me." I reminded him. Though, why I had to refresh his memory baffled me. His nonchalant attitude toward his powers also confused me. He clearly wasn't himself, his powers affecting me so easily being another clue.

"Oh yeah, that guy," he said with complete disinterest before turning away from the doctor altogether. He meandered over to Trisha's desk and started to flip through some of the papers on top of the desk.

Trisha quickly snatched up the files he had begun to scan and tucked them into her desk drawer with a sickly-sweet smile, "Nothing you'd be interested in."

"No offense meant," Sid held his hands up and stepped back from the desk, a smirk on his lips, "Just wanted to see what you ladies were up to the last few days."

"You know, same old same old," Trisha commented mysteriously enough it caused me to quirk a brow at her. She stared at me with such intensity I knew she was trying to tell me something, but I just wasn't getting it.

Leaning my hip against Trisha's desk, I crossed my arms over my chest and asked the strangely snoopy half-demon, "Why are you here?"

Sid turned his smirk to me, the affect that little quirk of his lips had on me was unreasonable. If this was what Sid's powers were always going to be like, we needed to get Asmodeus back on his side of the portal, and fast. I didn't think my heart—or libido—could take much more stress.

"You called me of course," Sid shifted toward me and I had to stop myself from backing away the way my whole body was screaming at me to do. Something wasn't right.

Trisha kept giving me a look, getting more exasperated and desperate by the moment, and I tried to figure out what she was trying to say. But I just couldn't read her.

"Right," I answered with a slow nod, "But you could have just called me back. You didn't need to come all the way over here." I made a show of going over to the coffee pot rather than letting him touch me again.

Apparently, my discomfort was not showing through because Sid came up behind me, his body heat pressing against my back making a shiver run through me. I grabbed the sides of the small table, holding the coffee pot and shook my head. Head clouded but body on fire, my two halves were at war with themselves. One side saying, 'touch him, kiss him', while the other side telling me to get as far away from him as possible.

"I know I could have just called, but I wanted to see you." His words breathed across the back of my neck and I spun around, not liking my back to him any longer. The move proved to be a bad idea because it put me face-to-face with the cause of my inner turmoil. And what a face it was.

"I wish you would have just called. We are pretty busy here," I argued, trying to get the conversation on point and not where it appeared to be heading.

"I know," Sid sighed and brushed a stray hair behind my ear. The single touch of his hand against my face made me close my eyes briefly. "You are so busy with your business and now the whole thing with Michael's dagger. I wish I could help you out more."

"It's fine," I said and then shook my head violently when I realized how breathless I sounded. What the hell was wrong with me? Clearing my throat, I side-stepped out of Sid's embrace, "I mean, we're fine. There's nothing you could do anyways."

"Are you sure?" Sid asked, following after me, "There has to be something. I mean, maybe I could hold onto the dagger for you? This way you don't have to worry about it so much."

Sid's offer to hold onto the dagger should have made me happy he was being so thoughtful, but all it did was fill me with suspicion. With the way Sid was behaving, having him hold onto the dagger would only make me more worried, not less. Besides, it was safely tucked away in the depths of the Phoenix guild.

"Don't worry about it. It's not here anyway," I commented.

Sid grabbed my arm, forcing me to turn around. His face contorted in anger as he practically yelled at me, "What do you mean it's not here?"

Eyes narrowed, I jerked my arm out of his grasp, "It's in a safe place. Why do you care so much anyway?"

"I don't," Sid replied quickly, his face smoothing out to a too-casual grin.

"It sure sounded like you did," Trisha said, the expression on her face now worried and I took a moment to study her hand as it clutched the edge of the desk. Her knuckles were ghostly white and her nails were biting into the wood. She was shaking slightly, her eyes darting from Sid to me repeatedly. Sid scared her. But why? He never scared her before.

Unless...

I turned my attention back to Sid and really looked at him. His hair was the same and other than his eyes being a more vibrant green, nothing about his face was different. He wore his usual tight shirt and dark pants, with his scuffed-up boots on his feet. He was missing something, though.

"Hey, where's your rosary at?" I gestured to his left arm where it was usually wrapped around his wrist.

Sid lifted his arm up and stared at it as if confused by my question. Then in a completely non-Sid movement shrugged, "Must have left it at home."

I exchanged a look with Trisha. Sid would never leave his rosary at home. Something was definitely not right.

"Hey Sid," I sidled up to him, my hand settling on the butt of my gun, "When's the last time you saw your father?"

"My father?" his brow rose in question, "Why are you asking about him?"

"Oh, I don't know. Maybe because his being on this side makes your powers wonky and I'm beginning to think it is lowering the effectiveness of your rosary."

"So?" he cocked his head to the side and gave me a boyish grin, "Don't you like me this way?"

The last time Sid had asked me the same question was when his rosary had been broken in this very room. He had showed up while I was in the middle of an exorcism, which in turn had caused his demon to act out. I had noted one thing from that day; Sid's demon was nothing to laugh about. And nothing I wanted to see again.

I was betting it was his demon side I was dealing with right now. It would explain my internal fight. It had happened the same way last time. While half of me wanted to kick his ass, the other half wanted to rub against him like a cat in heat. A particular mix of emotion which only came from the fact that Sid's father was the demon of lust.

I took a cautious step backward, not taking my eyes off Sid for a second. "Maybe we should go get your rosary."

"I don't need it," Sid growled, each step I took he countered until my back was to the wall. I didn't want to get cornered by Sid's demon half, but I also didn't want him anywhere near Trisha.

"I think you do." I snapped back and then said to Trisha, "Why don't you go get us something from the Chinese place Trish? I think Sid's going to be hungry after this."

Sid licked his lips, his eyes running up and down my form. "Oh, I can go all night."

"I'm sure you could," I muttered to myself and then said, "Still, Trisha doesn't need to be here for this."

"Oh, let the kid watch. She might learn something," Sid leaned in until I could feel his breath on my face.

I let out a forced laugh, "I'm sure she could. In fact, I hope so."

My words must have surprised Sid because his brows shot up, catching him off guard enough so he didn't see me twist sideways until my fist slammed into his face. He stumbled back, which allowed me to drop down and swipe my leg out, knocking Sid's legs out from under him. He grunted as he hit the ground. Before he could recover, I straddled his waist, my gun out of its holster and pointing at Sid's chest.

Sid stiffened as I pressed the barrel into his chest. "What the hell, Mary?"

I stared down at the half-demon beneath me. The bright green color of his eyes had faded back to the more hazel hue I'd grown to know. The creepy tingle began to subside and I relaxed slightly.

Sidney was back.

11

"MAN," TRISHA SAID, HELPING me get Sid into my bedroom, "What is it about today?"

"What do you mean?" I asked as I unlaced Sid's boots. I pulled them both off before sliding his legs underneath the covers. During the whole process, Sid's gorgeous eyes stayed closed.

The moment Sid had returned to his usual self he had promptly passed out. Since the couch was already taken, the only other place to take him to was my bedroom. While the prospect of Sid being in my bed would have been alluring, I didn't exactly find this situation mood-setting.

"I mean," Trisha tucked the pillow under Sid's head with a huff, "First, Doctor Ryan comes here and needs help, and then Sid shows up acting all funny. It has to be a full moon or something."

I glanced out the window. The sun shone in through the curtains and there wasn't a moon in sight. I turned back to Trisha with a confused expression, "I'm not sure what the moon has to do with it."

Trisha moved away from the bed with a groan, "Geez, Mary. It's like you're from another planet."

My brow furrowed at the comparison. "That's not far off actually." I glanced down at Sid; he wouldn't be going anywhere for a while.

I followed Trisha out of the office and into the living room where the doctor was still out cold. Our office had never felt so crowded. I had a sudden urge to take off, to leave this city, and start over. Somewhere else, someplace where neither human nor demon knew my name. Then maybe I could have some peace.

But then that would leave Trisha—and who knew who else—to clean up my mess. I had no doubt in my mind that if I skipped town, Asmodeus would take it out on those

I cared about it. Starting with the girl in front of me. The one I'd dragged into more than enough hostile situations. I couldn't do that to her, or any of them.

Sid would be alright for a little while. Asmodeus had shown he wouldn't truly hurt his son—maybe manipulate him and force him to be his demon side, but not hurt him. Though, I didn't see how letting Sid's demon side take control when he didn't want it free wasn't hurting him in some aspect.

I sighed heavily. Things were so much less complicated when I had been a mindless drone in heaven. I never thought I'd be craving that ignorance again. I let out a short laugh.

"What is it?" Trisha asked, stopping at her desk. She cocked her head slightly as she tried to decipher my thoughts.

"Nothing...just thinking," I shook my head and then smiled at her, "Anyways, we were talking about being from another planet."

"Yeah," Trisha crossed her arms over her chest and raised a brow, "You're not an alien, right?"

I chuckled and leaned against her desk, "Not in that aspect, no. But heaven isn't exactly on earth."

"Isn't it, you know," she pointed up to the ceiling, "Up there. In the clouds."

I gave her a knowing look, "Don't you think if heaven was in the clouds, your scientists would have found it by now?" When her face fell, I continued, "Heaven is higher up than earth but not in the physical sense." Trisha face scrunched together in confusion and I sighed.

"So, you know how I had to use Michael's dagger to make a portal to hell?"

"Yeah."

"That's because hell is another dimension. A lower dimension that earth is. And so, heaven…"

"Is on a higher dimension?" she finished for me.

"Exactly. So, there is heaven up here," I held my hand up at eye level, "and then hell is down here," I put my other hand at my waist.

"And then earth is right smack in the middle." Trisha put her hand in between mine.

"Right."

"So, we're like an earth sandwich." Her lips twisted in displeasure.

"I guess you could say that," I nodded and then waved hand at her, "Don't get me wrong. That doesn't mean our dimension is any better than your dimension. We just have more advantages than you do."

"But don't our souls go to heaven or hell when we die? How does that even work if we are in different dimensions?" Trisha sat down at her desk and crossed one leg over the other, her foot bouncing up and down as she thought.

"Well, like is attracted to like," I explained, turning so only my hip was resting against the desk, "When humans with good souls die, their souls or energies are released and drawn into our dimension. Since they aren't physical they can easily pass through the barrier. Unfortunately, that means the same thing for demons."

"Oh," Trisha drew out, "so that's why some demons can pass into our world without a portal but others can't. They don't have a physical form?"

"Correct. Only the upper demons, like Asmodeus, have a real physical form. The rest are just underlings who can barely survive in the hell dimension, let alone in your world. That's why they need to possess humans, and then, when I dispossess them, they become black smoke."

"So, do they go back to hell when you dispossess them?" The question hadn't come from Trisha, but instead from the other side of the room.

Trisha and I jumped up from where we sat, our eyes darting to the doctor. He sat on the edge of the couch, the expression on his face confirming he had been listening for longer than just a few seconds. Thankfully, his pallor had improved and the strength in his eyes said the extraction had worked.

"Good, to see you are doing better," I said, relaxing back against the desk.

"Thanks to you," Doctor Ryan nodded toward me, "I don't know how you did it, but I now know why you were so reluctant to donate your blood to science. While there might very well be a miracle cure in your blood, I wouldn't put my greatest enemy through what I've just experienced."

"Sorry." I frowned. What did you say to someone you had saved but who you'd also caused unbearable pain?

"No, no," Doctor Ryan shook his head and waved a hand in front of him, "No apologies necessary. You saved my life. If there was some other way to do it, I'm sure you would have tried it. Though, if I am honest, I didn't deserve your help."

Trisha snorted and I shot her a look. It was a strange turn of events that I was the one chastising her for being rude. Strange enough that I smiled.

"Don't worry about it," I told the doctor, "You can just owe me one."

"Several in fact," Trisha added and smirked.

"Of course, of course," the doctor stood from the couch and came toward us. "So, not only are you a savior of humans, you also exorcise demons?"

"Yes?" I drew out, watching the doctor as he scanned the small office waiting area.

"Doesn't seem to pay very well, does it?" his lips turned down and his brow furrowed.

"I get by."

Doctor Ryan's gaze landed on mine and he nodded once more. "I can imagine so.

You seem like a woman who can take care of her own." He paused letting an awkward silence fill the room.

Thankfully, Trisha broke it, "So," she turned back to me, "where do the demons go when you exorcise them?"

I let out a breath, happy to be able to discuss something I knew. "Most go back to hell to regain their strength. 'Cause like I said, it takes a lot of energy to come to this side whether you are physical or not. Sadly, some of the stronger ones will just find another host."

"Won't you just exorcise them again, though?" Trisha asked.

I chuckled. "I wished it was so easy. Most are smart enough to steer clear of me after that, so I can't exactly just keep knocking them off. I rarely meet the same demon twice." I paused and then said with a growl, "Except Asmodeus."

"Asmodeus? That name sounds familiar." Doctor Ryan pulled out his phone and typed something into and then his eyes widened slightly. "Asmodeus, demon of lust. As I'd thought." Trisha and I sent him questioning looks and Doctor Ryan chuckled, "Catholic upbringing. Somethings you don't ever forget. As a young boy, it was hard not to forget a demon with a horn for a ..." he stopped himself, his eyes darting to Trisha, before finishing, "in interesting places."

Trisha snorted, "Sadly, the picture doesn't match the real thing."

"Really?" Doctor Ryan asked, a strange kind of excitement filled his face, "What does he look like?"

Before Trisha or I could answer, a deep and familiar voice answered, "Like me."

We all turned to see Sid standing at the doorway to my office. My eyes scanned him, searching for any kind of clue his demon half was in control. When I finished at his eyes, all I saw was the hazel color I had grown to love.

"Don't worry, it's still me," Sid held his hands up in defense as he approached us.

"Is this the Asmodeus fellow?" Doctor Ryan asked, a hint of fear in his voice, "I thought this was your boyfriend? At least, that's what he said when he came to visit you in the hospital."

I shot Sid a look that said, "Really?" when I was in the hospital, Sid and I hadn't even been close to dating. Sure, we had kissed once, but that wasn't even close to where we were now.

Sid smirked but didn't try to deny it or defend it, instead, he answered the doctor, "Asmodeus is my father. I'm half demon."

"Oh," Doctor Ryan said as he visibly relaxed, "So, you and your father have quite a resemblance."

"Freakishly so," Trisha answered and shuddered.

Sid shrugged with an air of confidence, "What can I say, my good looks had to come from somewhere. And he is the demon of lust. Why wouldn't he be attractive?"

Doctor Ryan sighed, "Leave it to the Catholics to make lust into some disgusting monster."

"It is though," I interjected, "It's about moderation. Asmodeus isn't the kind of guy you want to jump into bed with. He wouldn't just show you a good time, he'll tear you to piece while you are begging for more."

"You say that as if you've seen it," Doctor Ryan's brow rose, a look of horror on his face.

"I have," I stated simply. Leaving it at that, I turned to Sid, "We should get your rosary before your bad side rears its ugly head again."

Sid shook his head, "I don't even know where it is."

Trisha moved closer to me as she asked, "How exactly did you lose it in the first place?"

Sid rubbed the back of his head and frowned hard, "I don't know. Last thing I remember was leaving Mary at her car after our botched date, and then heading for the bar. When I got there, my normal crew wasn't there and the bar was empty."

"Strange," I commented. On a Friday night, even early in the evening like it would have been when he'd arrived, there should have been some patrons already drowning their sorrows from the work week.

"Then, the next thing I know, you are above me with a gun pointed at my chest." Sid's brow raised, the look on his face telling me he wasn't exactly unhappy about the position we had been in.

Ignoring the look, I turned to Trisha, "Why don't you help Doctor Ryan home and then stop by the bar and see if you can find the rosary. It's likely still there."

"Who do you think removed it?" Trisha asked, gathering up her keys and purse.

I thought back to the one other time Sid had gone full demon on me. It had been Asmodeus who had been able to put the rosary back together. So, if he could put it back together he could probably remove it just as easily. Question was, why would he want his son full demon now?

"My bet would be his father. But why?" I turned my attention back to Sid, "Any ideas?"

Shaking his head, he tucked his hands in his pockets. "Your guess is as good as mine. I can only figure he meant for me to be a message of some kind, since I ended up here. Maybe he wanted to threaten you into taking the charm off him."

If Asmodeus thought he could get me to do what he wanted by threatening me and mine, he had another thing coming. I'd learned the hard way he wouldn't let them go free just because I did what he wanted. I was getting tired of playing by his rules. This time I'd go to him.

12

BEFORE TRISHA HEADED OUT with the doctor, she pulled me aside. Confused by what she might want, I waited for her to say her bit while the men waited on the other side of the room.

"Look, you are a grown woman and everything," Trisha started causing me to smile slightly, "but you are going to be alone with our dear Sidney in a place with a bed."

"Yeah?" I cocked a brow, "Your point?"

"I'm just saying," she shifted uncomfortably, "I've been where you are, emotions get heightened and feelings start to emerge. Next thing you know, you're on your back in the back of a musty caddy, losing your virginity to the Starbucks guy."

"Starbucks guy?" I grinned, "What are you getting at Trisha?"

Sighing, she patted my arm, "I'm just saying be careful. Don't do anything you don't want to do. He's half human, but he's also half demon. Demon of lust, demon. Meaning he can easily make what you feel amplified. I don't want you to do something you might regret later."

I leaned down until my forehead touched hers, "Don't worry. I'm an angel. The likelihood of me letting him seduce me with his powers is low. Besides," I smirked, "I have handcuffs and a gun. What's the worst that could happen?"

"Sounds like the beginning of every bad porno to me," Trisha muttered, the worry still on her face.

"Trust me, Trisha. All clothing will stay on our bodies until the world isn't on the verge of ending." With a small smile, I bumped a fist against her shoulder.

Returning my look, Trisha said, "If you say so, but don't come crying to me when things get out of hand and you can't find your underpants."

Pursing my lips together, I forced back the laugh threatening to be unleashed. Instead, I turned back to the room where Sid and Doctor Ryan were watching us with great interest. Shaking my head at Sid's questioning look, I ushered Trisha toward the door.

"Remember what I said, Mare," Trisha warned with a serious stare before she led the doctor down the stairs shutting the door behind her.

"What was that all about?" Sid asked when we were truly alone. He stood close enough to me that my nose filled with his masculine scent.

"Just girl stuff," I remarked moving into my office. I needed to put some distance between Sid and me. I hadn't even been thinking about how things could get physical between Sid and I while Trisha was gone, but since she'd put the thought in my head, it seemed to be all I could think about.

I went to the mini fridge and pulled out a bottle of water. I chugged the water, hoping the cool liquid would lower my temperature. Sid had followed me into the room and sat on the edge of my bed; I could feel his eyes boring into my back.

"What?" I asked, turning around after I finished my water.

"You tell me." He put one foot up on the edge of the bed, his eyes focused on me. There was confusion there, but also a bit of humor. He seemed to think my actions were funny for some reason. Probably because I was acting like a scared lamb. Which I wasn't. Archangels weren't afraid of anything, let alone the prospect of having intercourse.

Intercourse. Sex. Screwing. Boinking. All the different names of procreating didn't make a difference to me. I was in the dark no matter what. The only experience I had was the one-time Sid and I had fed his powers and learned that angels could indeed have an orgasm.

Just thinking of that time made me shudder.

"Angel," Sid said in a tone that pulled me out of my thoughts. His eyes had darkened and his breathing heavy.

Uh oh.

"What are you thinking about?" he asked, standing from the bed and prowling toward me like a lion seeking out his meal.

Gulping, I forced myself not to take a step back. To show him weakness might set his demon side off. Just thinking about what had happened with us before, had already begun pushing him to that edge. I needed to get him off it, not closer to it.

"Nothing. Just something Trisha said," I replied and cursed myself for the breathlessness in my voice. Sounding turned on would not help the situation.

"And what did our girl say?" Sid prodded, coming up to me, his hand trailing down the side of my arm making my skin burn where he touched.

"She was worried," I gasped as both of his hands landed on my arms. Somehow—maybe the lack of his rosary—caused the sensation of his touch to zip straight through me and into places they shouldn't be.

"Worried about what?"

Clearing my throat, I shook my head. This couldn't happen. We needed to restrain his demon half, not provoke it. "Nothing. She was worried about nothing. Just silly human stuff."

"I'm a human. At least in part," Sid said, coming in closer to me, "It might not be silly to me."

"How long do you think we have until your demon half rears its ugly head?" I asked, trying to change the subject.

Surprised by the question, Sid's brows raised, "I don't know. I've never gone this long without the rosary. Even with it, he's hard to control when I haven't fed in a while."

A thought occurred to me then. "When was the last time you fed?"

My question caused Sid's face to shut down. From his expression, I could tell he was thinking hard. Harder than he should have been regarding something he was so religious about. I took a step further away from him and more toward my desk. I had the cuffs in there, as well as my spare gun. I had stupidly left my other one on Trisha's desk.

"Sidney," I said, pulling his attention back to me, "When was it?"

"I don't remember," he said at last. There was a torturous look in his eyes that pulled at my heart, and almost made me go to him, but I stopped myself. If Sid didn't remember the last time he had fed then his demon half could come back out at any moment, and he wouldn't hesitate to take what he wanted.

"Then we should take some precautions," I stated, holding the cuffs up as I clutched the spare gun in my hand. It didn't have holy bullets in it but the regular ones would slow him down enough to get away if the need arose.

Sid's eyes locked onto the gun and then to the hand-cuffs. Instead of reacting the way I would have hoped—in a rational manner—his lips curved into a seductive grin. "If you wanted to play games, angel, all you had to do was ask."

"This is no time for jokes, Sidney," I snapped, my grip on the gun tightening, "Your father is out there somewhere, probably waiting for this exact thing to happen. But in his mind, it would go down a completely different way than how you and I wanted it. And no offense, but I'm not dying today."

I lifted the gun and pointed it at Sid who had begun to close in on me. I didn't want to shoot him. I wasn't sure if he could heal as easily as I did, even with regular bullets. But if it came down to me or him, I would always choose me.

"Come now, angel," Sid maneuvered around the desk, his fingers trailing the glossy metal surface, "you don't really want to shoot me, do you?"

"Not if I don't have to."

"And you don't have to," he responded, moving in closer until the barrel of the gun pressed against his chest, "I'm still me. I'm not him yet. We can stop him before he ever gets close to the surface."

Frowning at his explanation, I asked, "How?"

Raising a brow, Sid stared at me, "You know how."

Of course, I did. It had crossed my mind briefly, but only for a moment. Then I had squashed the thought because there was no way I was putting myself in a vulnerable position where Sid's demon half could kill me. No matter if it might stop him.

"No way," I shook my head and shoved the barrel of my gun into Sid's chest with a bit more force, "You just stay on your side of the room."

"Mary," Sid growled, his hand reaching out and grabbing the gun before I could blink. He tossed it behind him without much effort, "I can feel him. He's hungry, and he likes your fear."

"I'm not afraid of you," I snapped, taking a step back. My hip hit the window-sill, and I turned so I wasn't caged against the wall.

"No," Sid agreed, "but you are scared of him and how he will make you feel while he does horrible things to you."

He wasn't wrong. I'd seen the crime scenes, I knew what his father could do. I didn't think it was a coincidence that father and son shared the same looks; more than likely they shared the same tastes too.

"You're right, I don't but unless you can fight him off there is a high chance that I'll have to use my powers on you and I don't know what that would do to you." I pleaded with him, trying to make him see reason. I didn't need a gun to fight demons, all I needed was me, but that part of me didn't know restraint. All it knew was to destroy the evil and it didn't care who got hurt in the process.

"You need to help me feed, Mary. It might be enough to keep him back until Trisha returns," Sid tried to convince me, the desperation in his voice making me pause.

"So, like before?" I asked, my legs banging against the edge of the bed.

Sid shook his head sadly, "No, not like before. That won't be enough this time," his hands curled into fists in front of him, "I need to be inside of you...he needs to be inside of you. Even if he doesn't get you the way he wants."

I gulped at his words. This wasn't the way I'd wanted my first time to go down. I'd never even thought much about how it would happen. Not until Trisha and Sid had put those silly human thoughts in my head. In heaven, sex was just a way to procreate. Nothing more. Pleasure wasn't at the top of our minds, let alone the desire to make sure it was special.

But now, I didn't really have a choice. I could try and keep him distracted long enough for Trisha to get to the other side of town and back— not likely to happen. Or I could go for the gun and more than likely end up shooting him—which could kill him. I really didn't want to do that either.

Or.

Or I could suck it up and satisfy the beast. Some would see it as a win-win, but Sid and I would only see it as being forced to do something that should have been precious to us. Doing it this way would make it tainted, and it always would be tainted.

"Fine," I said finally, "I'll do it."

"Excellent," Sid's mouth curled up into such a satisfied look I was worried that maybe the demon was closer to the surface that he had let on.

Sid tried to close in on me but I put my hand up to stop him, "One condition."

"Of course," Sid held his hands out to the sides, "Anything the lady asks."

Ignoring his chivalrous act, I snapped, "I'm on top."

13

NOW THAT I'D AGREED to do the deed, a wave of shyness come over me. I hadn't been this out of my comfort zone since I'd had to learn to fly.

I was what they called a late bloomer. While angels were born with wings, we didn't know how to fly right away. Which meant we had to learn. My teacher was Zachariel. Hard as nails, he didn't give a shit about fears.

I was an angel. I was born to fly, and having a fear of heights was not something they had ever even heard of.

It was safe to say flying school hadn't been a pleasant experience for me; a requirement, not a pleasure. Kind of the same thing as this situation.

While, I wanted to be with Sid in this way eventually, I'd never imagined it would be like this; with him sitting on the edge of the bed and me anxiously trying to get the nerve up to actually do the deed.

"Relax, angel," Sid tried to soothe me, placing his hands on my shoulders, but I shrugged them off, "You're going to have to touch me."

"I know," I snapped, and then flushed, "Sorry, I mean, I know," I sighed and sat down next to him on the bed, "I know what is supposed to happen, but actually doing it is a completely different thing."

We sat there for a few moments and then Sid said, "I don't want to rush you into this, but we don't exactly have the luxury of time."

I crossed my arms over my chest and glared.

Sighing, Sid inched a bit closer to me. I forced myself not to move away, and waited stiffly to see what he'd do next.

"We don't have to jump right into it," Sid cupped my face in his hands, "We can start slow. It'll draw it out...make the feed that much better. He'll like that."

"Oh, so it's about what he'll like now?" I said through clenched teeth.

"Mary," Sid angled my face up to his, "Just trust me. I won't let it get out of control. I promise."

I blew out a breath. "I'm sure you say that to all the girls," when Sid gave me an exasperated look, I sighed, "Alright, alright. I agreed to this. I guess my moaning and groaning is just going to make it worse."

Sid raised a brow and smirked. "Oh, there will be moaning," he leaned down and pressed his lips to the side of my neck making me wiggle, "and groaning," he opened his mouth, placing the hot surface of his tongue along the vein in my throat, "But they won't be in displeasure."

"Okay." I gasped sharply as he sucked hard on the junction of my neck and shoulder. My arms dropped down to my side and I leaned into him letting him direct me so his arms were on either side of me. His chest pressed against mine and my nipples hardened into peaks as they brushed against him.

He tried to ease me back onto the bed but I froze. Sid pulled back with a questioning look. I shook my head and said, "I won't be on the bottom. The chances of him coming out during the act is too high, and I won't be torn to shreds like those women were."

Sid paused for a moment and then nodded and moved back. I let out a breath and stood from the bed. Now that I was in charge, I wasn't sure what to do. Sid had been trying to get me in the mood and to stop thinking about it so much, and while it had been working I now had to keep it going.

"Angel?" Sid asked when I took too long to do anything. My gaze shot to him sitting on the bed and I scanned his clothes. We both still had them on—at least for now—and I realized I was about to break the promise I had made to Trisha.

I scoffed, "What the hell," I untucked my shirt and chunked it over my head, leaving me in a pale pink bra Trisha had helped me pick out once upon a time. My hands went to my pants and I started to undo the buttons when Sid's hand stopped mine.

"What are you doing? Let's just get this over with," I tried to move my hands but Sid wouldn't let me.

"We might have to do this because of my father's tricks but I'm not going to let him or my demon side ruin this for us." Sid's eyes met mine before he lowered his head down. His lips brushed mine and my hands dropped to settle on his hips. Sid moved my hands aside and unsnapped my jeans, then slowly unzipped them as his mouth pressed to mine.

I opened my mouth to his, allowing the taste of him consume me. He pushed my pants down over my hips and I stepped out of them. Usually, nudity didn't bother me, but standing there in just my underwear while Sid kissed me, I felt unsure. Breaking the kiss, I ducked my head down, my hands going to his waist. If I was going to be undressed, then so was he.

Sid gaze scorched against my skin as I slid my hands underneath the bottom of his shirt. My fingers tickled along the surface of his skin making him take a sharp breath. I knew how he felt. I, myself, was having a hard time breathing.

"Angel." Sid gasped out as my fingertips skimmed just underneath the top of his pants. I unhooked his belt and unsnapped the button. The sound of his zipper as I pulled it down filled the room, setting something inside of me on fire. Suddenly, I couldn't get him unclothed fast enough.

No longer going at a slow pace, I jerked his shirt up and though I'd meant to pull it over his head, instead I ended up ripping it in half. Sid let out a short laugh, his lips curving up in a delicious smirk, "Impatient?"

I gave a shaky laugh and then dragged a hand through my hair. "Maybe. I've never done this before."

"I know." Sid's tone making my eyes jerk up to his. The desire was still there but there was something else too; a softness that wasn't there before. Before I could ask about it, Sid ducked his head down and captured my lips. Our mouths molded together and my hands wrapped around his waist. My bare chest pressed against his, pulling a soft sound from me.

Sid's hand moved down my back, trailing along my skin. I shivered in response, pressing myself closer to him. His hand dipped lower, over my backside, and settling between my thighs. Molten fire ripped through me and I jerked back from Sid's kiss, a startled cry falling from my mouth.

My eyes locked with Sid's, the green and gold mixture of his irises were bright and seared into me. A kind of male satisfaction covered his face; it felt as if he were challenging me. Never let it be said I was not up for a challenge.

I stepped back from Sid, whose brow rose in question. Lips ticking up, I shot out my hand, shoving Sid away from me and onto the bed. Flat on his back, his hot gaze followed my every move. It made me put a bit more of a sway in my hips, a sense of confidence filling me. This might not be the ideal way I wanted it to happen, but it was happening but my way.

Climbing onto the edge of the bed, I crawled up Sid's body my mouth pressing to the muscles of his abs and chest before I straddled him. Hands splayed out on his chest, I settled back against him feeling the hot length of him against my backside.

"What are you going to do now, angel?" Sid's hand cupped my hips and squeezed slightly, "I'm at your mercy."

I gave a throaty laugh, my head thrown back, my back arched. It caused a physical reaction in Sid that pulsated against me. Rolling my head back down, I licked my lips, "Are you now?" I moved back slightly causing my heat to slide against him.

Sid made a choking sound and gasped, "Yes. Whatever you want."

Hands braced on Sid's expansive chest, I pushed myself up slightly and then reached between us. I didn't bother asking about protection. One good thing about being an angel; human diseases didn't really catch. And pregnancy? The likelihood of being able to procreate with a half-demon was slim to none.

As I sat down onto him, all thoughts flew from my mind. A hot pressure stretched inside of me, causing my mouth to open wide and my breath to catch. Sid's grip tightened on my hips as if he were struggling as well.

"Are you alright?" Sid gasped, his jaw clenching tight.

Swallowing thickly, I nodded but still didn't move. It was an unusual feeling; one I had never felt before, a fullness I'd never imagined. It kept me frozen in place, not able to go any further.

"What's wrong?" Sid's expression turned worried and his thumb stroked my hip bone. I shuddered at the feeling, causing

Sid to groan beneath me. Curious at his reaction, I shifted again. Sid's grip tightened on me once more. "I won't be able to hold back if you keep doing that, angel."

"You mean this?" I rocked my hips a bit more aggressively, and this time the movement caused me to groan. That was different. An achiness started deep inside of me, a curious feeling which made me move tentatively again. The same feel began again but when I tried to stop once more, Sid wouldn't let me. He pulled me back and forth and it took all I had not to cry out.

My hands flexed on Sid's chest as I asked, "And I thought that was all there was to it."

Sid smirked at me his eyes hooded, "You haven't seen nothing yet."

14

THE PHONE RANG NEXT to the bed a while later. I rolled over and released a groan. With each movement, a delicious ache settled low inside of me, reminding me of what I'd just done.

Picking up the phone, I glanced back at my bed-mate. Sid lay on his stomach, one arm thrown over the side of the bed. Though I was the one who'd been fed off, it seemed Sid was more exhausted than me.

While today's events were not how I would have expected them to go, Sid had made sure his demon half was kept at bay long enough for us to enjoy ourselves without worry. I frowned. At the end though, there had been a moment when his eyes had flashed bright green and I'd thought I might be in trouble. But Sid's back had arched slightly, his mouth open wide as we met our mutual completion.

Turning my attention away from my new lover, I looked to my phone. Trisha? Why was she calling?

"Trisha, hey. Did you find Sid's rosary?" There was a pause on the other end of the line and a choked sob. "Trisha? What is it? What's wrong?" I jumped to my feet searching around for my clothes. Sid shifted in the bed. As I pulled my pants on his eyes opened.

The moment he saw my face his brow furrowed, "Mary, what's wrong?"

"I don't know." I shook my head and then said into the phone, "Trisha you have to talk to me. I can't help you if you don't tell me what's wrong."

Deep breaths came through the phone and after one last shuddered breath Trisha rasped, "I...I got the rosary."

"You did? Great!" I turned slightly to Sid, "She got your rosary." I grabbed my shirt off the ground and pulled it over my head. Sid climbed out of bed and began to dress himself, sans his shirt since I had pretty much destroyed it.

"So, where are you?" I asked, and then with a frown, "and why are you crying? Did you have a fight with your mother again?"

"No. No," Trisha said, her voice still thick with emotion, "Not my mom."

"Then what is it?" I exchanged a look with Sid who wanted to know what was going on. I shook my head, telling him not now.

"Can you just come get me?" Trisha asked in a tone I didn't like at all.

"Sure," I answered, my brow furrowed, "Where are you?"

"I'm downstairs." Trisha finally answered after a moment's pause, "I'm at Madame Serena's."

Somehow the way she said it made my stomach twist. "I'll be right there." Hanging up the phone, I grabbed my discarded gun from the ground and headed for the door.

Sid grabbed my arm before I could leave. "Something's wrong," I shook my head and met his eyes, "I don't know what it is but I could hear it, in Trisha's voice."

"Then I'm coming with you."

My eyes went to his bare chest and I smirked, "I'd say alright, but I think you'd be a bit of a distraction."

Sid glanced down at himself and then took a step toward me, that sexy knowing smile of his spreading across his lips, "You think so?"

His hands gripped my hips, but I put my palms up to keep him from bringing us together, which only cause me to touch the warm surface of his skin. Something pulsated inside of me; a reminder of what we did just a few moments ago. I swallowed thickly, but still pushed him away.

"After we help Trisha."

"You're right," Sid nodded and then glanced around the office, "You don't happen to have a spare shirt, do you?"

I chuckled, "As much as I'd love to see you try and fit into one of my shirts, you'll just have to wait." My smile disappeared as I remembered how Trisha had sounded on the phone. "I don't want to leave her alone for too long."

"Alright. Be careful though. It might be one of his tricks." Sid didn't need to say the demon lord's name for me to know he was talking about his father. The thought had occurred to me that Trisha's reactions on the phone could be a ruse. A trap to get me to come downstairs, and with Sid balancing the fence of good and bad guy, I couldn't very well bring him as back up.

I made it down the stairs and paused just before the door. Peeking out the window of the security door, I searched for any sign of Asmodeus or his goons, but the street in front of our building was deserted. There wasn't even the usual handful of cars parked at Lou's Chinese.

Inching the door open, I held my gun in my other hand, ready for any demon who might jump out at me. With no one on the sidewalk, I shoved the door open and strode the few feet to Madame Serena's door. Trisha wasn't outside the shop, so that meant she had to be inside the eerily quiet place.

The open sign still glowed, but there were no customers in sight. I pulled the door open and the bell at the top of the door dinged. The instant my foot touched the ground, I knew my gut feeling had been right.

Demons had been here.

The shop reeked of demons; every inch of the place was drenched in it. My stomach rolled against the scent of it in my nose but I forced myself to move forward. Trisha had to be here somewhere.

I didn't have to search much. I rounded a bookcase and found her hunched over something in the corner. Trisha's shoulders shook, her sobs making my heart ache.

Taking slow cautious steps over to her, my eyes snapped to the figure on the floor.

The pale grey of the carpet next to the form had turned a dark brown color. And beneath the scent of demon was the reek of death and dried blood. Madame Serena.

I dropped to the floor beside Trisha. I reached out to brush the dark hair away from her face. The pale terrified face of Madame Serena stared back at me. Sighing, I placed my hand on Trisha's arm.

She turned her face toward me slightly, the tear tracks down her cheeks had smeared her make-up and she resembled a raccoon more than a human. "Was it him? Did he kill her?"

My lips pressed into a thin line as I turned my attention back to what had once been Madame Serena. Asmodeus's other victims died with a smile on their face. Madame Serena sure as hell didn't look like she had been enjoying herself. The cuts along the surface of her face, and her torn nails told me two things. They had tortured her, and she had fought back. Adara would be happy to know that.

Dammit. Adara. I was going to have to tell her. Rage spread through me at the thought. The bastard had done this on purpose. Asmodeus wanted me to know he could get to me. That's why he had picked Madame Serena. I didn't think he knew she was the one who had made the charm because if he had, I doubted he'd have let her die so quickly. He'd have made his goons bring her to him.

"No," I sighed after a moment, "He didn't do it personally, but I'm sure it was one of his goons. The place reeks of demons." I rose to my feet, searching for some other sign that might tell me differently, but I found none. "It's too much of a coincidence. First, Sid coming, his missing rosary, and now this?"

"Oh yeah," Trisha said her voice small and then dug into her pocket. She pulled out a beaded necklace with a cross at the end and handed it to me. "Here, it was on the floor of the bar. I doubt he got more than two feet in before they took it from him."

"Did anyone stop you?" I asked, taking it from her.

"Just that bartender," Trisha said with a blush on her face even with the death before us. She wouldn't look me in the face as she said it so I couldn't exactly not poke at her.

"You mean the vampire who had the hots for you?" I offered her a small smile and then started for the door. Before I reached it, I paused, "I need to tell Sid."

"Where is he by, the way? I would have thought he'd be permanently attached to your side," Trisha said, catching up to me.

This time it was my turn to blush. "He's...uh...not fit for the public right now." Trisha smacked me on the arm, hard enough for me to flinch. "What the hell was that for?"

"You totally slept with him, didn't you?" Trisha screeched before she started to pace.

"Trust me Trisha. All our clothes will stay on our bodies. I'm an angel, there's no way I'll just let him seduce me. Isn't that what you told me?"

"I know, I know," I held my hands out in front of me, "I broke my promise but I didn't have a choice."

"Is he still alive?" Trisha huffed.

I placed my hands on Trisha's shoulders, "He was slipping away. His demon half has gotten too strong since his father crossed over. I did what I had to do to stave off the monster inside of him."

Trisha stared down at the ground for a moment and then a smile crept up on her face, "So, how was it?"

Dropping my hands, I scoffed, "Like I'm going to tell you."

"Oh, come on," Trisha whined and stomped her foot like a petulant child, "I've been rooting for you guys to do it from the beginning and now that you've finally done it, I don't even get the nitty-gritty details? So not fair."

"Is this really something we should be talking about right now?" I glanced back to Madame Serena's body and swallowed hard.

Trisha followed my gaze and licked her lips. "I need to think of something else right now. If not, I'll fall apart and I'm tired of being the one who ends up crying."

"I understand but I'm still not telling you." I gave her a pointed look and started for the door again, and then once again stopped in my tracks.

"What is it?" Trisha asked from beside me.

"Adara. I need to call Adara. This has to end." I pulled my phone out of my pocket and pressed the number for the ex-demon hunter, my heart in my throat as her voice came over the line. "We need to meet. Meet me at Madame Serena's and bring the dagger."

15

AFTER I HUNG UP with Adara, I went about closing Madame Serena's shop. Most people would have called the cops and been sure not to touch anything. But I wasn't most people. And this wasn't some random attack.

Sure, Thompson would have understood a demon attack, but he'd feel obligated to file a report and go through all the right channels. Which would mean lots of red tape to cross and testimonies to give. Things I didn't have time for.

Adara's guild—the Phoenix hunters— were used to handling this kind of situation. Also, with Madame Serena on their payroll to watch me, I figured they would want to take care of their own.

I pulled the string on the neon open sign, turning it off for the last time. A sense of melancholy came over me at the action. People kept getting hurt around me, Trisha more than once. The list of humans who had died because of the demons I faced were too many to count. And now, Madame Serena, who had been nothing but kind to me.

My lips quirked up as I thought of her awe of Uriel. At least now she would be with the angels she adored so much. Gaze shooting to the ceiling—though I knew it wasn't how it worked— I said a silent prayer for them to take care of her. It wouldn't reach them, but it made me feel better and with Adara walking through the front door I needed to be strong.

The moment she stepped into the shop I could tell she knew something was wrong. She might not have been an angel but her awareness had evolved enough to sense when a demon has been there. Her dark hair, pulled back in a long braid down her back, exposed her throat as she swallowed several times. You never get used to the smell of demons. Once you became sensitive to them their stench permanently fills your senses. I was sure Adara and I would both be taking a cleansing shower tonight.

"What happened?" Adara demanded, striding toward me in her five-inch-heeled boots. I'd never learned how she could handle walking around in those all day, let alone fight in them. It did bring a certain kind of seductive quality to her ensemble; deep red leather pants, and a long-sleeved black top made of some kind of silky material. When she turned slightly to take in the rest of the room, I could see the bare back of the shirt, held together only by a few tiny strings, her phoenix brand on full display across her back. Dangerous and sexy, a lethal combination I was sure she had used to her advantage on more than one occasion.

"Adara." There must have been something in the way I said her name because she stopped dead in her tracks before turning her path toward the back of the room. "Adara!" I yelled after her trying to catch her before she found the body.

Five-inch heels apparently didn't make her any slower than me and she reached the body first. Collapsing to the ground next to Madame Serena, Adara made a strangled noise in the back of her throat. Trisha and I had closed Madame Serena's eyes and had taken the tablecloth from where she performed her psychic readings, covering her up to the neck. Adara lifted the cloth and gasped at the damage beneath.

Dropping the cloth, she turned to me abruptly, her eyes shining with unshed tears of anger. "When?"

I shook my head, "I don't know. Things have been pretty crazy for me, I didn't hear anything at all." I explained to her about Doctor Ryan and then Sid. Adara sat there listening without a word. She didn't even make a comment about how Sid and I had finally consummated our relationship.

"We have to make them pay," Adara said between clenched teeth. Liquid fire burned in her eyes as she glared down at Madame Serena's face. Asmodeus's goal might have been to threaten me, but had had an additional side effect. He'd made and enemy of one of the most feared Phoenix hunters in North America.

We both rose to our feet as Adara pulled out her phone. She dialed a number, shouted some orders into the phone and then turned to me. "Thank you for calling us first. The guild is indebted to you."

I nodded, "No problem. I figured you'd want to handle it without the cops getting in the way."

"You're right." Adara glanced down at Madame Serena once more. There was so much anguish in her expression, and I didn't understand it. I thought Adara was just someone she'd hired to keep an eye on me, but now I wondered if maybe the old woman had been something more to my friend.

Since she didn't offer up the information, I didn't ask. She'd tell me when she was ready. We had more important things to worry about than her precarious relationships.

The bell above the door went off and my hand went to my gun. Adara grabbed my wrist and my gaze went to her. "It's just the cleanup crew."

Cleanup crew? It sounded so cold and clinical. Like Madame Serena wasn't anything but trash to take out. But now, I guess that was all she was. Her soul had long since left her body, and though I hadn't checked her soul lately, I was sure she had gone the right way out of this dimension.

"Where's Trisha?" Adara asked as we watched a few uniformed members of the guild survey the area, taking a few pictures here and there. I opened my mouth to answer her, but waited as they began to load Madame Serena up into a body bag.

"They'll study the wounds back at the lab to find out what kind of demon killed her," Adara answered my unasked question before asking me once more, "So, where is everyone?"

I led Adara out of the shop behind the cleanup crew. We headed over to the door leading to my office and made our way up the stairs. "Trisha and Sid are both up in the office. I decided to wait for you down here so...in case..." I trailed off, letting the words hang in the air.

"I flipped my shit?" Adara finished for me.

I cast a weak smile behind me. "Pretty much."

I'd only seen Adara in action once, and the fact that she hadn't burned the building down around us had been more than surprising. I'd have been lying if I didn't admit to being bit excited to see her come up against Asmodeus and his goons.

"Hey, you're back," Trisha greeted me as I walked through the office door. When she saw Adara behind me, her face fell. "Adara, I...I'm really sorry."

Adara wrapped her arms around my assistant giving her a tight squeeze. She had always been more touchy-feely than I was. I wasn't surprised when she hadn't greeted me the same way.

"Thanks so much for being there," Adara said before releasing Trisha with a grin, "We're going to get those filthy demon leeches," her gaze darted to Sid who had just entered from my bedroom, "no offense."

Sid held his hands up, "None taken. I'm with you." His eyes locked with mine and the hate in there surprised even me. I didn't know he hated his father to that extent. Then again, we hadn't really talked much about his family, or what had happened to him in the past. This wasn't the first time his father had used him to do his bidding; who knew what else Asmodeus had done to him? Just thinking about it made my heart ache for him, and the need to tightly wrap my arms around him was almost too much to resist.

Instead of following through, I turned to Adara and asked, "By the way, did you bring it?"

Reaching into her boot, Adara pulled out the dagger that had started it all. Flipping it over in her hand, she held it out to me hilt first. Taking it from her, I gripped it tightly in my hand.

Asmodeus had done enough damage for the short time he had been in this world. It was time for him to go back to where he belonged, this time for good.

16

"THAT'S YOUR PLAN?" ADARA crossed her arms over her chest with a disbelieving scowl, "They kill Madame Serena—a sweet woman and a damn good psychic—and you just plan on sending them all back to hell?"

Pressing my lips into a thin line, I returned her look with one of my own. "What else do expect me to do? I can't kill them all. Asmodeus, sure; he's in his physical form now, but he has dozens of demons following him."

"That didn't stop you from rushing in on him before at the hotel," Trisha pointed out even as I glared at her.

"This is different. They had a hostage then. This time, there's no deal, no reason to be cautious. We get in and get Asmodeus, and then get out again.

Hopefully, before he can surround himself with all of his cronies."

"Once we get my father, then what?" Sid asked, his eyes burning with anger, "We can't just hand him over to the police."

My lips curled up, "Who said we were going to?" I withdrew Michael's blade and flipped it in over in my hand, "He wants this blade so bad, we're going to give it to him."

"So, are we going to bring him back here?" Trisha asked looking around the office, "It's not really set up for torture and death," she blanched shooting a look to Adara, "Sorry."

Adara shook her head, "Don't worry about it. Serena would have wanted her death avenged, and don't worry about the location," she turned her attention to me, "I've got a place we can take him."

"I thought you were out of the game?" I cocked a brow at her in surprise.

"Just because I took myself out of the hunt doesn't mean I stopped being a hunter. Being prepared is part of the life." Adara gave me a lethal grin, sending a chill down my spine.

"Wait a minute," Trisha held her hands up, putting herself in the middle of our little group, "So, the plan is to get Asmodeus," she looked to me and I nodded, and then she moved her gaze to Adara, "Then take him to your place where we do whatever it is we are going to do."

"Right," I said, placing my hand on the butt of my gun. My veins were pumping with excitement just talking about getting rid of Asmodeus. He had been a pain in my ass for far too long, and I was happy to finally get rid of him.

"So, can someone tell me where Asmodeus is?"

The silence following Trisha's question caused my excitement to stall. None of us had even thought of it. Other than Asmodeus's little message with Madame Serena and the sudden attack on Sid the demon lord had yet to show his face. I had no idea where he'd decided to hide out at now.

Turning to Sid, I raised a brow, "Any ideas?"

Sid rubbed his jaw on which a five o'clock shadow had begun to show up. After a moment, he sighed in frustration. "I don't know. He hasn't contacted me since we left the hotel. He likes nice things," Sid met my eyes, distress in his expression, "He wouldn't want anywhere too populated."

"That's obvious," Adara rolled her eyes, "No demon wants to draw attention to himself, but I think I can make a few calls and find out if there's been any new demon activity," Adara pulled her phone out and started punching in numbers, "Give me a few minutes."

While Adara chatted away on the phone, I turned to Sid and glanced down at his rosary. "Are you doing alright? Will you be able to handle this?"

Sid rubbed the rosary with his thumb and frowned. "I'll be fine. I'm tired of being his pawn. I want a normal life," he smirked at me, "or as normal as it can be being what I am."

"I know how you feel," I slid my hand into his and gave it a squeeze. Sid leaned down and pressed his lips to mine without deepening it. He released me after a moment, shooting a look at Trisha who wasn't even trying to give us privacy. She wiggled her brows at me and I stuck my tongue out at her.

"Alright. I got a lead," Adara said stepping back into our circle, "There's more-than-normal demon activity on the north side of Priscal Ave. Which happens to be near a newly-foreclosed property. Who wants to bet that's where our demon lord is hiding out?"

"Sounds good to me. When do we go?" Trisha bounced on her heels, her eyes darting around the circle.

"You aren't going anywhere," I snapped, causing Trisha's expression to drop.

"Come on, Mare!" Trisha cried out, throwing her hands down in frustration, "You can't leave me out of this. I deserve revenge just as much as any of you." she gestured wildly to Sid and Adara, "Even more so since I have actually been at the mercy of his delightful hands."

Trisha scowled, a darkness filling her eyes. I didn't need to be psychic to know she was remembering the time Asmodeus had taken her. I had saved her before she had become one of his victims, but only just. Who knows how much tormenting she had endured before I'd gotten to her?

"I understand," I placed a hand on Trisha's shoulder. The look she gave me when she looked up would rival any demon's. She really wanted her shot at Asmodeus and probably thought I had robbed her of it.

"Do you really, Mary?" she snapped, though her anger was halfhearted, "Sure, he's threatened you, and maybe his goons have hurt you, but you don't understand what it's like to be human. To be helpless like I was. It's the worst thing I have ever felt."

"Trisha," I said sternly, forcing her to stop her rant. "I'm not telling you you can't get your revenge," Trisha opened her mouth to argue but I cut her off, "I'm saying you aren't going to help us capture him."

"Which means..." she drew out, this time not quite catching on to what I was saying.

Adara laughed and threw her arm around Trisha's shoulders. "What she's saying is you are going to get your pound of flesh, my dear girl. But after we deal with the demon horde."

"Really?" Trisha's eyes lit up as she turned back to me.

"Yes," I nodded with a soft smile, "I wouldn't want anyone to rob me of my revenge, why in the world would you think I'd prevent you from getting yours?" I shook my head as I realized we were having a mushy moment over torturing someone. Trisha's mother would have a cow.

Sid cleared his throat breaking up our moment. "While, that's all good and all, I'm afraid I'll have to make a detour before we go raiding anywhere."

My brows furrowed, "What do you mean?"

He lifted his arm—the one holding the rosary—and shook it. "If you expect me to be of any help and not suddenly jump sides mid fight, I'll need to stop by St. Michael's Cathedral and have my rosary reblessed."

"I thought you said you were fine." I stepped up to him, placing a hand on his arm.

Sid gave me a grim look, "Physically yes, but inwardly, I can feel him fighting against the rosary's barrier. I might be fine for a few days, if I was just going to work and the like, but going up against my father?" he crossed his arms over his chest and stared down at the ground, "I don't know if it will withstand his powers. He's easily removed it before. What's stopping him from doing it again? I'd just feel better if I got an extra boost in case something happens."

I studied Sid and realized he was right. We needed all the help we could get, and we couldn't risk things going to the shitter if he suddenly went demon on us before we could even take his father down. His father had been able to get to him before, what was to say he wouldn't again?

"Alright," I agreed, causing everyone's attention to turn to me. "Sid's right. But you aren't going alone." I didn't give him the chance to argue. "Your father took the rosary from you once already, I won't let it happen again. We don't know if he has men watching you. They could be waiting outside this very moment for you to be alone and do what he did again."

Sid looked like he might fight me on it, but after a moment he closed his mouth and nodded tersely. "Very well. But it has to be you."

"Fine," I turned my attention to Adara, "While we are getting his rosary powered up you take Trisha to the location you have in mind. Get her ready for when we come back. Things will move quickly and we can't afford any slip-ups." I looked to Trisha and asked, "Can you go down to Madame Serena's and help Adara find a book on demon-binding spells?"

"Sure," Trisha nodded, her brow furrowed, "But what for? If we are just going to kill him?"

"And you think he's just going to sit there and let us?" I let out a dark chuckle, "Demons might be gluttons for punishment but not that much. I highly doubt Asmodeus will leave this world without putting up one hell of a fight."

"I agree," Adara stated, then grabbed Trisha by the arm, "We are going to need a few things, and if I know Serena she'll have it all in her shop," Adara ushered Trisha toward the door, then stopped and turned to me, "Be careful. I wouldn't want to lose you too."

My lips quirked up at her concern, "Don't worry, you can't get rid of me that easily."

We clasped hands tightly, our eyes locking before she and Trisha were gone. I let my gaze follow them for a while, committing their faces to memory before giving Sid my full attention. "Are you ready for this? In and out, that's it. No detours."

Sid smirked at me before drawing me close, "The only detour I'll be making is to send as many demons as possible back to hell."

17

ONE WOULD THINK DEMONS couldn't enter a church—even a half demon—but demons loved nothing more than to commit sacrilege. Sid must have worried he'd be burned on the doorsteps when he'd first come to the church. Then again, I didn't know a huge amount about his history.

"Sid," I said as I followed him into the overly elaborate church. At least this one didn't have stone statues.

"Yes?" he answered, on his knees before the line of candles set for prayer.

I stood by his side, my eyes searching out any unexpected attack. "How long have you known you were part demon? Or have you always known?"

Sid's head jerked up from where he prayed, "Why the sudden interest?"

I shrugged, "Your disdain for your father was one telling sign. While I understand not wanting to be used, I can only imagine some of your hatred had to come from somewhere else," an unidentifiable emotion flickered across his face before it was gone again, "Something happened, didn't it? To make you hate him so."

Sid sniffed and then smiled briefly, "Doesn't it always?"

Placing a hand on his shoulder, I pressed him to continue.

"You don't want to hear my sad and unfortunate story," Sid stood from the floor and faced me, "We have a demon lord to capture."

"And he'll still be there when we are done," I stopped him from trying to bypass the question. Sid stared down at flickering flames of the candles, his fingers wrapped tight around the rosary. A priest hadn't been available to bless it, but a dip in the holy water should be enough to keep the demon side of him at bay.

197

"My mother wasn't like his other victims. He didn't kill her while he raped her, nor did he give her to the lower demons." His words were low and so full of pain I almost made him stop, but since I had pressed him for it, it didn't seem right to stop him.

"She was beautiful, my mom. With a kind heart and a sharp tongue. I'm not surprised he found her intriguing enough to take her to hell as his wife."

I swallowed hard at this knowledge. A demon's bride was truly a cursed creature. One who would endure unimaginable torment and pain? For Sid's mother to have survive long enough to have had a child meant she'd either had a strong soul or a stubborn one. Sometimes the two went hand-in-hand.

"You didn't grow up in hell, though?"

"No," Sid shook his head, "Thankfully, not. Mom," he paused and sighed, "she cared for me as much as she could for someone who had a literal demon for a spouse. She was not much more than a slave, and treated worse. But she promised to get me out of there. She didn't want me to be raised by such an evil creature with such disregard for living things." His eyes burned hotter than the flames of the candlewicks.

"What happened to her?" I asked in a quiet voice, even though part of me almost didn't want to know. For the emotion in his eyes to be so violent, it must have been something gruesome.

"She died...obviously." Sid gave a short laugh. I didn't see how it was funny. At my confusion, he continued, "One day she found a portal the demons were using to bring humans slave in and out of hell. She stalked the portal until she knew exactly when it would be unoccupied and safe to use.

"While a slave to my father, she was still the demon lord's wife, and her position gave her some privileges and respect the other human slaves didn't have," he gave me a small smile which only made me frown harder. I didn't like where this story was going. "Long story short, she incapacitated my father long enough to grab me and make it to this world."

"That still doesn't answer how she died." I tried again, his story not really making sense.

"See, that's the funny bit," Sid shook a finger in the air at me, "She had been in hell for so long, suffered so much abuse, her body had become weak and fragile. We hadn't been back more than a few days before she fell ill and died from pneumonia."

I made a noise in the back of my throat, not believing what he had said, "Wait, what? That can't be how it ended. You're messing with me."

Sid shook his head and scuffed his foot against the tile floor. "I wish I were. I wish I could say she turned into a badass demon-hunter like Adara and took down all those who had abused her, but sadly it wasn't the case," his face became serious once more, "She died and I was sent to a Catholic

Orphanage, where I learned fairly quickly how to use religion and God to stave off my other self," he released me and clapped his hands together, "And that is the end of my tragic tale."

"Not quite," I bumped him on the shoulder, "You still have a few chapters left to get your revenge. For you and your mother."

Sid leaned down, pressing his forehead against mine. He closed his eyes and took a deep breath. I held onto his waist and waited for him to gather himself. I'd made him delve into some deep stuff. Most people wouldn't want to relive their worst memories, but he had done it for me because I had asked him to.

"Thank you," he said after a moment, his words shocking me.

"For what?" I asked, leaning away from him, "I haven't done anything but get you in trouble since we met."

Sid smirked and chucked me under the chin, "If I didn't have you around to get me in trouble, I'm sure I'd have found another way, but the chances of me surviving would have been a lot lower."

I chuckled and shook my head, "Don't sell yourself too short. There are few who I'd trust to have my back other than Adara and you."

His fingertips slide along the edge of my jaw, drawing my head up, "That has to be the sexiest thing you've ever said to me."

"Says the son of the demon of lust." I breathed in as his heated stare scorched my insides. His face came closer to mine, but before his mouth could take mine a buzzing in my pocket interrupted us.

Ugh.

I pulled away, holding a finger up. "Hold that thought," withdrawing my phone from my back pocket, I frowned, "What's up Trisha?"

"Hey, just wanted to let you know a whole butt load of cops are outside the shop right now. Adara says she thinks someone must have seen Madame Serena and the cleanup crew and they are probably here to arrest us.”

“Shit.” I ran a hand through my hair, my mind going a mile a minute. This was the last thing we needed. We’re supposed to be storming the castle and defeating the monster, not dealing with the authorities. As I took a deep breath, I heard talking in the background on Trisha’s side. “Listen, do as they say and as soon as you get to the precinct, ask for Thompson, or a lawyer. Don’t do anything to show your guilt.”

“Alright, Mom. Will do,” Trisha said, confusing me for a moment and then I realized the cops must have come in.

“Be careful. I’ll be there as soon as I can,” as I hung up the phone, I turned to Sid, “We should get going. Trisha and Adara have been arrested. They’ll probably find us next.”

Pulling away from Sid, I placed my hand on the butt of my gun and kept an eye out, this time for cops. I never imagined I’d be on the wrong side of the law, especially for something I didn't do. If Asmodeus had anything to do with this, I was sure he was laughing his head off right now.

Sid and I marched down the aisle, full of purpose as we made our way to the front door. I thought of going out the back but it would have seemed too suspicious. Besides, it wasn't like anyone but Trisha and Adara knew where we had gone, and I was sure they wouldn't tell.

My thoughts derailed as I pushed open the church doors to come face-to-face with a parking lot full of cops and a truck full of SWATs.

Then again, how well do you really know people?

"Mary Wiles," Detective Riley stepped up on the steps of the church, his gun pointed at me, "You are under arrest for the murder of Sansa Brian."

"Who?" I asked, Sid and I exchanging an equally confused look.

Riley sighed, but kept his eyes hard, "Madame Serena. Come quietly and no one needs to get hurt."

I took my hand off the butt of my gun and dropped my arms to my side. The whole squad seemed to tense at my movements, making me wonder who had been talking to them. Coming down the stairs, "I have to say I'm a bit flattered you thought you needed this many people to capture me." I smirked and gestured around us. I felt Sid come down the stairs behind me, stopping as I paused before Riley. "Didn't think you could handle me on your own?"

I probably shouldn't have been poking fun at him, but since the accusations were unjust I didn't seem to be taking the whole thing too seriously.

"We have it on good authority to be wary of your tricky ways. As of four forty this afternoon you are one of LA's most wanted."

"Most wanted?" I raised a brow and looked back to Sid with a grin. "Did you hear that Sid? We're wanted."

"Not him," Riley gestured to Sid with his gun, "Just you. He has nothing to do with this, unless you are saying otherwise?" his gaze locked on mine, daring me to make things worse for myself.

"No, you're right," I replied, "Sid has nothing to do with this. Here," I held my hands out to him, "I'm all yours."

"Really?" Riley cocked a brow, hesitating for a moment before shaking it off. He gestured to one of the uniforms, "You heard her. Cuff her and put her in the car."

As they put the cuffs on my wrists, Sid touched my shoulder, "Are you sure about this?"

"Don't worry about me," I shook my head, "Go home and wait for my call," I locked eyes with the detective, "This won't take long."

18

IT WAS A STRANGE feeling being the one with the cuffs on. As I was led through the police station doors, the secretary didn't greet me with a cool disregard, she went about her business-like people she knew got arrested every day. Some cops stopped and stared as I was led through the open office area; they too surprised to see me as the one under arrest. I hadn't worked with every cop in LA, but most of them at least knew me by name, if not by face.

One thing hadn't change. The demon-possessed criminals lined the wall, waiting to be processed. Except this time instead, of hissing and cursing my name, they smiled in glee. For once, the big bad angel was just as bad as them. Well, I had news for them, I wasn't guilty and doubted I'd stay long.

Adara and Trisha were somewhere in the precinct, though, I doubted Riley would let me see them. Probably didn't want us to have a chance to send some kind of secret message. Not that we had any to exchange.

Hopefully, Trisha had done the smart thing and hadn't called her mom. Thompson would be the only one who could help us. Adara, I didn't have to worry about. This wasn't her first rodeo. The guild had their own lawyer and her dad wouldn't let her go down for anything, let alone the death of one of their own. Problem was, we'd still have to suffer the insufferable bullshit which came from being suspected of murder.

A female officer started patting me down again when I arrived. They had already taken my gun and briefly searched me before putting me in the car, but they had missed Michael's dagger in the top of my boot. This cop didn't. She slid the blade out, staring in awe at the elaborate handle and blade. The moment it was out in the open the demons cried out and flinched, as if it would strike them down.

"Knock it off," Detective Riley shouted and then turned to the cop who had frisked me the first time, "How could you miss a knife that big, Morgan? She could have gutted us all!"

"Sorry, sir. It won't happen again, sir," Morgan mumbled before stumbling away.

I didn't even bother to try and keep a straight face. No matter what I said or did, Detective Riley had it in for me and he was going to get his pounds worth.

"What the fuck are you smiling at, Wiles? You're in here for murder!" he yelled in my face before gripping me by the forearm and roughly yanking me out of the intake area.

Detective Riley took great pleasure in escorting me through the precinct as if I were a prize cow being shown off at the fair. He paraded me through the desk area and into an interview room. The last time I'd been in there with him he had made some not-so-very-nice suggestions about me and how I got the police to do what I wanted. I didn't suspect this time would be any different. I hoped Thompson arrived soon.

Riley promptly cuffed me to the metal table in front of us, as if he thought I was going to jump across the table and attack him. I couldn't say it hadn't occurred to me but that would only make me look more guilty.

"Oh, how the tables have turned." Detective Riley lips curled up into a nasty grin. He had a folder in front of him and he wasted no time opening it up to toss out photos. Madame Serena's face looked back at me, her eyes. But some of the pictures were up-close-and-personal views of the damage the demons had done to her.

"I knew you were some kind of crazy, but I never expected you'd be into mutilation," he shook his head and rocked back in his seat.

I stared across the table, waiting for him to ask me a question. He glared back, probably expecting me to react to the photographs. I wouldn't give him the satisfaction.

"You don't even care, do you?" Detective Riley dropped his chair to the floor and pointed at one of the photos. "This woman was your landlord. You saw her almost every day and you couldn't give a fuck that you and your sick girlfriends murdered her!" he threw the photograph at me, and it hit my face before floating down to the ground, "Did you guys enjoy it? Did it turn you on?" he sneered, "I bet you fucked right there next to her corpse like the sick fuck you are."

"Are you done?" I asked calmly.

Detective Riley's face turned red and his seat flew back hitting the wall as he jumped to his feet. He was around the table and in my face in a matter of seconds. "Am I done? I'm going to show how done I am." His hands reached out to grab me by the front of my shirt before the door swung open revealing a stranger; a man I didn't know.

"That will be enough of that." On the far side of fifty, his greying hair was combed precisely over his balding head. His keen eyes zeroing in on Detective Riley hands on my shirt. "Are you manhandling my client?"

"Client?" Riley's grip loosened slightly before he let go of me altogether. "Your client brutally murdered her landlord in cold blood and then tried to cover it up!"

The man—apparently my lawyer—strolled into the room and stared hard at the detective. "You have nothing but the word of an eyewitness who you have yet to disclose. What your eyewitness saw was Miss Wiles and her associates doing as they were told by the FBI; to quietly cover up a serial murder. Now," he cleared his throat and gestured to my handcuffs, "If you could release my client, we can all get back to work."

Growling in frustration, Detective Riley unlocked my cuffs chucking them to the side. Before I could get up he slammed his hand down on the table and leaned in close. "This isn't over bitch."

The childish side of me couldn't help the grin on my face, "Looking forward to it."

I followed my savior out of the interview room and into another office where Sergeant Thompson, Adara, and Trisha waited.

"Mary!" Trisha cried out wrapping her arms around my waist. I placed my hand on the back of her head and hugged her back as I nodded to Adara and Thompson.

"Your father is quick," I noted, jerking my chin at the lawyer, "I half expected to be here overnight."

Adara shrugged and grinned, "For all his faults, my father knows when to make things a priority. Keeping us out of jail, and the cops off the demon murder, is one of them."

I let go of Trisha and turned to my savior, "Thank you for what you did back there, Mister…?"

"Mayer. Patrick Mayer," he shook my hand, giving a slight inclination of his head,

"I am happy to help someone of your stature, Miss Wiles," his greying brows bunched together, "Can I call you Miss Wiles, or would prefer your angelic name?"

"Angelic name?" Thompson's eyes widened, his words not much more than a whisper.

Patrick's face sobered as he quickly added, "I apologize. I thought everyone in this room was up to date on your celestial status."

I waved Patrick off, "Don't worry about it." To Thompson I said, "I'm an angel. I lost my wings, so I'm technically not one any more. Get over it." I turned to Adara and cocked a brow, "FBI?"

Shrugging a single shoulder, Adara rolled her eyes, "It's my father's go to for any murders that are demon related, especially if they have gotten compromised."

"We have several FBI agents all around the world," Patrick filled them in, "It is quite easy to have them draw up some paperwork for this case. Enough that even Detective douche-bag would be satisfied."

"Douche-bag?" Trisha giggled, "That's what we call him too!"

Patrick smiled slightly, "Well, the name is appropriate." He turned to Adara, a kind of reverence in his gaze, "If you have no further use of me I will be going. I'm sure you can keep yourself from being arrested for the rest of the day?"

"I'm sure we can handle it," Adara held her hand out to the lawyer, "Thank you once again for saving my ass."

"Always a pleasure," Patrick shook her hand and then nodded to the rest of us before heading out the door.

"You're an angel?" Thompson pointed an accusatory finger at me.

"Yes."

"Okay. Alright," he took slow deep breaths as he seemed to come to terms with my lineage. After a moment, he turned to Trisha and Adara, "Are you angels too?"

"I wish," Trisha moaned, "Then maybe my mom would stop riding my ass."

Adara chuckled and then held her hands up, "Ex-demon hunter and human as they come...mostly." She and I shared a knowing smile.

"Good," Thompson sighed, "I can only handle one revelation at a time. Get out of here before more people start asking questions. You can pick your weapons up at the front."

"Thanks Thompson," I mock saluted, earning me a head shake from the sergeant.

The exit of the precinct was a bit like the entrance, except this time the police officers were in awe for a different reason. Probably how quickly we were released. I made a rude gesture to the demons who hissed at me as we passed.

As Adara and I retrieved our weapons, Trisha flipped through her phone. Even though Adara hadn't hunted demons in a while she still kept a small arsenal on her. A short sword down the spine, two small handguns on either hip, knives on the wrists and then an even small knife in her boot. Seeing her tuck her knives into her boots, reminded me I was short one.

Michael's blade.

"Hey," I turned to the officer working the front counter. "I'm missing one. A dagger. About four inches long, an inscription on the blade."

The officer looked down at his form and then shook his head, "I don't have a blade written down and there's not one here. You'll have to take it up with the officers who brought you in."

Frowning, I exchanged a look with Adara and Trisha. They seemed as worried as me. The missing dagger was a bad sign. I had a feeling who would have taken it, but I marched back into the precinct and found the female officer who had taken it off me.

She shook her head and claimed not to have any memory of such a blade.

Dammit.

If I hadn't suspected before, I knew now without a doubt someone had taken it. And by someone I meant of the demonic nature.

"Our plans are not ruined," Adara assured me, "We don't need the blade to get to Asmodeus. We can still make this work."

"I know, but it would have been poetic to kill him with the same blade he was so hell bent on getting his hands on." I sighed and pulled out my phone as we headed for the door. Hopefully, Sid was still at the church, or better yet, had taken my advice and gone home.

The voice on the phone told me otherwise, "Hello, Muriel. I believe you have been looking for me."

19

"YOU KNOW, YOU HAVE more drama in your life than a soap opera," Adara started as we were going over our inventory of weapons at her secret warehouse. It wasn't so secret anymore now. Since Trisha and I knew where it was located. While Adara and I prepared, Trisha had decided to scope out the place. Wanted to make sure it would be private enough that no one would hear Asmodeus's screams, or so she said. I thought she might need some time to come to terms with what we were about to do.

Of course, this meant Adara would take this moment to ask me about my love life.

"What makes you say that?" I cocked a brow at her.

"While I'm happy you've finally gotten some," she glanced at me while adjusting her wrist sheaths, "Why did you have to pick a guy who keeps getting kidnapped?"

Loading a utility belt with extra ammo, I snorted, "I thought you'd be proud; he is half demon. Isn't that part of your niche?"

Adara rolled her eyes, "Just because I like a certain flavor to my sex does not mean I have a niche. And when I told you to find someone to rock your world, I didn't mean you had to find the first demon who gave you the look."

"The look?"

She sighed and waved her hands in front of her, "You know, the I-want-to get-in-your-pants look. There are plenty of men who have given you the look, you just haven't noticed."

I chuckled at her description, "I wouldn't know it if they were. I was completely oblivious to Sid until recently," I shrugged and then gave her a flat look, "If it took the son of the demon of lust to get my body to respond, I don't think any normal human would do it."

"If you say so," she raised her hands in defense, "But you shouldn't knock it until you try it."

Frowning, I snapped the last bit of weaponry in place, officially labeling myself as armed and dangerous. "I appreciate your concern, but what's this really about?"

"What do you mean?" Adara said, avoiding my eyes as she loaded her pistol.

"You never had any issues with Sid before and now you are all about trying to get me to drop him. What's up?" I crossed my arms over my chest and leaned against the work-table beside us.

"Nothing," she shrugged and picked up another case of ammo. Where she was going to put it was beyond me; we already had more than a small army's worth of weapons and ammo between us. Still, with Asmodeus, we could never have enough.

"Come on. When have you ever not told me what's on your mind?" I bumped her on the arm as I tried to get her to open up. No need for us to have issues just when we are about to go into the lion's den.

Adara finished getting ready while I waited beside her, not giving up on getting a straight answer. After a few moments, she finally caved. Giving an exaggerated sigh, she turned to me. "Demons just aren't who you settle down with. They are great for a good time, and definitely when you want to orgasm, but other than that they are nothing but trouble. Hasn't Sid already proven that?" she pointed a blade at me before tucking it in the sheath on the back of her pants.

My mouth turned down as I processed her words, "So, you think I shouldn't date Sid. That I only have intercourse with him?"

"Yes."

"This coming from the woman who left her family, and way of life, for a demon," I snapped becoming defensive.

"That's different," Adara retorted, "Bernard was a vampire and he didn't try to kill me as Sid has already done with you,"

222

she held up two fingers with a scowl, "Twice."

Not wanting to argue anymore, I moved away from the bench and started for the door. Pausing on the threshold, I looked over my shoulder, "Do you have my back or not?"

Adara sighed and rubbed the back of her head, "Of course, I do. I just don't want you to get hurt. Keep in mind Sid might not to be saved this time."

"Then I'll deal with it. Either way, we have to stop Asmodeus," placing my hand on the butt of my gun, I squeezed until it bit into my palm, "And this time, he won't get away."

* * *

THE HOUSE ASMODEUS HAD taken for his own was a lot nicer than I'd expected.

For a demon, who had holed up in a warehouse and then a hotel room, this was a difference I didn't mind. No elevators to ride, nor any boxes to maneuver through.

"I say we round the house and take the guards out one by one," Adara gestured around the house as we sat in the car a few houses down, "Then we can sneak in the back door and take them all by surprise."

"Or," I drew out, "since Asmodeus is already expecting us, we go through the front door." I opened my door and then stepped out before Adara could answer me.

"Mary," Adara jogged up beside me as I crossed the street, "We can't just go through the front door. What about the element of surprise?"

"There's no need," I argued, "We need to get in there and find out if Sid has been turned again. Then we can decide if this is a rescue mission, or a capture mission."

Adara frowned at me in the dim lighting of the street lamps. "But what about Sid?

Are you just going to leave him there if his demon side has taken over again?"

I nodded reluctantly, "Unfortunately, taking on Sid's demon and taking out Asmodeus is not something we are going to be able to do by ourselves. If we had the whole guild backing us up then I'd say we could try for both, but since it's just the two of us," I gestured between us, "I don't see how it's possible."

"Not anymore," a voice from behind us said.

Adara and I spun around, each of us drawing our weapons. When my eyes landed on Ramiel—with his hands raised to show us he wasn't armed—I lowered my gun.

"What are you doing here?" I asked, putting my gun back in its holster.

"I've been watching this house since after our argument," Ramiel explained. His eyes had the intense focus he usually had when we had an important mission. "There has been a high level of demon activity in the area and it all leads back to this house.”

“How do you know that?” Adara asked. She still had her knife and gun out, having not even lowered it when we’d realized it was Ramiel. Did she think Ramiel was a threat too?

Ramiel met Adara’s questioning gaze with one of his own, “Did you think I spent this whole time just messing around? Like Muriel,” he nodded to me, “I too have been trying to take out the demons plaguing this city,” a frown marred his face as his eyes searched out around us, “It’s uncanny how so much evil can congregate in one place.”

“Yeah,” I murmured, “Uncanny.”

Ramiel’s explanation didn’t do anything for Adara’s expression. She still had the look of someone facing down a potential enemy. For all I knew she was right. Ramiel had fallen but how far has yet to be seen.

“How do you think you can help us?” Adara asked her gaze searching over Ramiel’s form. “You don’t even have a weapon. You won't be able to help against a feral dog, let alone a nest of demons."

A sly grin slid over Ramiel's face as he reached back behind his neck and withdrew a long broadsword. We hadn't even seen it hiding at his neck.

Seeming to read my thoughts, Ramiel smirked and twirled the sword around in his hand, "Just because I'm fallen doesn't mean I don't still have some of my powers. You of all people should know this, Muriel."

"Mary," I corrected automatically and then sighed. I looked to Adara, "We could use his help and three is always better than two."

"Unless, he turns on us mid-fight," Adara offered up her eyes locked on Ramiel.

"There was always that chance with Sid coming with us as well," I reminded her, and then turned back to Ramiel. "Alright, here's the deal. We are going in there outnumbered and without the element of surprise. Asmodeus is already expecting us, so there's no need to waste time beating around the bush with this."

"What's the goal?" Ramiel asked, already getting into mission mode.

"Search and capture," I replied and shot Adara a warning look when she made a noise in her throat. "Asmodeus is weakened by the charm we put on him back when he captured Ramiel, so he shouldn't be a problem. But getting past his demon goons might be," I sighed and then added, "And his son might end up on his side. But if Sid's on our side, we are to rescue him as well."

"What do you mean?" the confused expression on Ramiel's face made me hesitate, but then I shook it away. Why did I care what Ramiel thought? He was already fallen; there wasn't much lower he could go.

"Sid is a half demon, but he isn't just Asmodeus's son, he's also my…" I paused, not sure how to explain it. Sid and I hadn't even gotten to the labelling part of the relationship. "Sid's my friend and we can't leave him if we can save him."

To my surprise, Ramiel didn't question my explanation. He simply nodded.

"Alright, good. Everyone ready?" I waited until I received confirmation from both of them and then said, "Let's go."

Turning back toward the house, I drew my Glock and took a breath. I didn't think Asmodeus would attack me the moment we stepped in the house. He wouldn't have answered Sid's phone and invited us there had he not wanted something from me. Apart of me wondered if I was making a huge mistake.

My doubts aside, I led us across the lawn and up the stairs. Pausing at the door, I wondered if I should knock, or maybe ring the bell? I didn't have a chance to decide because Adara came up beside me and— with one swift kick—knocked the door in.

Lips twisted into a grimace, I stared hard at her.

"What?" she shrugged, "I wasn't going to wait here all night."

Shaking my head, I gestured for them to follow me. Breaking the door down must have notified someone of our arrival. Just because Asmodeus knew we were coming didn't mean we should let our guards down.

As we walked through the dark living room and down a long hallway, a horrible feeling began to churn in my gut. Where was everyone? Not a second later, Adara voiced my concerns.

"I don't like this," Adara murmured beside me. I nodded briefly, not taking my eyes off the walls around me.

The hallway took a sharp left and then there it was—a light at the end of the hall, shining from beneath a set of double doors. My hand tightened on the butt of my gun, my shoulders tensing in preparation for an attack.

Adara and I exchanged a glance as she hovered on one side of the door. Ramiel stood at my back. When Adara signaled she was ready, I reached for the door handle. Twisting the knob, I pushed both doors open and stepped into the room, my gun leading the way.

Unlike the rest of the house—which was barren of any furniture or life—this room was full of chairs and couches, all of them were filled with demons. They gave sharp-toothed smiles and chuckled as my mouth dropped open slightly.

Closing my jaw with a snap, my eyes narrowed on the one laughing demon at the head of the room. Sitting in a highbacked chair with one leg crossed over the other was the demon of lust himself. It was unsettling how much he and Sid looked alike. Sid, though, wouldn't be caught dead in a tailored suit.

At the moment, Sid was nowhere in sight. "Where's Sid?" I asked, the barrel of my gun never wavering from the head demon's form.

Leaning on the arm of the chair, Asmodeus tapped his chin with his finger.

"Hm, he was around here somewhere. Now, where did that pesky son of mine go?" he glanced around the room exchanging a laugh with his demon-possessed human lackeys.

All eyes went to another door to the room as it opened and revealed Sid. His bright-colored eyes and lack of rosary told me I would find no help in him. He glanced at me briefly, and then at his father to whom he inclined his head, before leaning against the far wall.

Damn. So much for saving him this time around. We'd just have to go forward with the original plan. Asmodeus was the primary target. Sid was just a bonus. But at the thought, a fist tightened around my heart.

Thankfully, I didn't have time to think on it as Adara and Ramiel stepped into the room behind me. Adara's shoulder brushed mine but Ramiel stayed back and to the side, almost as if he didn't want to be near us.

Pushing the stray thought aside, I gritted my teeth, "I'm not playing games with you anymore. Where is Sid and where is Michael's blade? I know you took it," I pointed an accusing finger at Asmodeus, who had the gall to be confused.

"I don't know what you are talking about Muriel," he smirked at me, "I've been here with my fellow demons this whole time, ever since you and my son lassoed this damned charm on me." Asmodeus reached under his shirt and pulled out the charm Madame Serena had given me.

Thinking of Madame Serena and how she had died caused my anger to rise. "Don't fuck with me Asmodeus. I'm tired of your crap and your lies. You are going to pay for what you did to Madame Serena and all the other lives you have ruined."

"What is she babbling about?" Asmodeus asked, but it wasn't the demons he questioned, nor Adara either. No, his eyes were firmly locked on Ramiel.

Ramiel stepped forward, shrugging his shoulders with a sheepish grin. "What can I say? I got a bit carried away."

Asmodeus clicked his tongue and shook his head, "You angels, give you a taste of evil and you start killing people left and right."

Adara and I stared at the exchange, our mouths wide open. What the hell? Ramiel was behind Madame Serena's death? The look of horror on the psychic's face flashed through my mind and rage I had never known before rushed through me.

"You?" I pointed a finger at Ramiel, "You killed Madame Serena? What did she ever do to you?"

"Nothing," Ramiel shrugged, then gave me a grin, "She was in the way and now she isn't. I couldn't very well have her contacting anymore of our kind. Uriel always was a nosey little bitch. If she found out how to get rid of the blade then it would ruin all of our plans. Oh, by the way," he reached into his boot and flipped out

Michael's blade. "I believe you were wanting this." He strolled through the room of demons without a care, and handed the blade, handle first, to Asmodeus.

Hot flames burned my eyes as I glared at him. All this time, I'd known something was wrong with him. I knew he had fallen, but not how far. Now, I knew.

"Mary," Adara warned from beside me, but I didn't acknowledge her. My mind had already been made up. Without warning, I shifted the aim of my gun from Asmodeus and pointed at one of the demons on the couches. I didn't give them a chance to process anything as I squeezed the trigger in quick succession. Taking out four demons before the others stood to attention.

Adara didn't say a word. She withdrew her own gun and began firing, taking out the rest of the demons as I strode across the room. My focus narrowed down to Ramiel and Asmodeus. The two who had done everything possible to ruin my life, and the lives of everyone I cared for.

Ramiel—the reason I ended up trapped on earth in the first place—and Asmodeus, whose only crime was being exactly what he was, a demon. For that reason alone, he needed to die.

Just a little bit more I thought, filling my clip once more and then withdrawing the knife from the sheath strapped to my thigh. Inches away from my goal, I caught a movement out of the corner of my eye before I was knocked to the ground. Struggling against the attacker, my eyes shot to his face.

"Sid!" I cried out, forcing myself not to shoot him, "This isn't you...you can fight it."

"I know, and I am," Sid assured me in my ear causing my eyes to widen in surprise, "I'll explain everything later, but right now you have to pretend to knock me out."

Pressing my lips into a thin line, I tried to figure out Sid's game but decided if something was finally going the right way, then I wasn't going to question it. I whipped my gun out and swiped it against the side of Sid's head. He winced and gave me a disappointed look before falling unconvincingly to the ground beside me.

Not sparing Sid another look, I searched out Asmodeus and Ramiel. Horror filled me as my eyes settled on the two of them in front of a gaping hole. Michael's blade! My gaze shot to the blade currently in Ramiel's grip. He and Asmodeus grinned like fiends as the portal opened before them.

Gritting my teeth, I shot to my feet and barreled toward Asmodeus. I wouldn't let him, or anyone else, use the dagger to bring more demons over. I shouldn't have even given it to him the first time around. The charm had been a bandage to fix my mistake, but now the bandage wasn't worth it because Asmodeus had still found a way to cause havoc, even without his powers.

It was finally time. I had saved it up for so long, not using it when I'd really wanted to, even when there were demons I'd felt had really deserved it. But now, all my waiting would be paid off. I reached inside of me for the core of my holy powers and drew it up until it warmed my palms.

I extended my hands, my eyes firmly on Asmodeus's neck. I could almost feel him beneath my grasp. I would enjoy watching as he burned away into a pile of dust and bone. Maybe I would keep him in one of those urns humans were so fond of for keeping their dead. Then I could put him on my shelf as a sort of trophy!

Before my hands could wrap around Asmodeus's neck, another paler neck jumped in the way. My eyes locked with Ramiel's but it was too late. My power had already come to the surface and I couldn't pull it back now.

The holy power filtered out of my hands and into Ramiel. I didn't even have a chance to think that perhaps it wouldn't work on him, when his face began to disintegrate before me. I ripped my hands back from him, only faintly aware of the dagger dropping to the ground as his hands crumbled.

Asmodeus didn't miss it fall though, the moment it landed he scooped it up. Jerking away from what was once my former commander, I grabbed at Asmodeus but using my holy powers had weakened me. The demon lord shoved me aside easily. I collapsed to the ground, a sudden wave of weariness taking hold. I could only watch as Asmodeus rushed into the portal, dagger clutched in his hand.

"Adara!" I cried out, searching for my companion. She stabbed a demon through the heart before turning to me. Her eyes widened and she rushed to my side.

"What happened?" her eyes darted around us, "Where's Ramiel and Asmodeus?"

I glanced to pile of dust next to me and then to the portal which was closing quickly. "Their gone and Asmodeus has the dagger."

"Then let's go after him," Adara started to get up from the ground, but I grabbed her arm weakly.

"No, wait. You can't go in there. You won't survive on your own," I tried to explain as fast as I could. I could feel the darkness closing in. There was always a price to pay when using my holy powers and it was coming to collect.

"Then, I'll have to go," Sid stepped up beside us. He shot me a reassuring look but there wasn't enough time for anything else because the portal was almost closed. Before I could try and argue, he rushed through the hole and then...nothing.

20

I COULD HAVE BEEN out for hours, days, weeks, and I wouldn't have known it. Using my powers had finally caught up with me. My brain and body had been short-circuited by using the bulk of my holy powers, leaving me little more than a vegetable.

During this time, I didn't dream. Or if I did, I don't remember. Probably for the best. The things in my dreams tended to hurt more than reality did.

Eventually, I began to flicker in and out of consciousness, picking up stray voices and bits of conversation here and there.

"How is she, Doc?" Trisha asked from where she sat at my side. I tried to open my eyes, but they were so heavy I couldn't manage lifting them. If opening my eyes was such a challenge, then thinking I could reach out and touch her was completely ridiculous.

"It's hard to say," a voice I recognized as belonging to Doctor Ryan responded, "With a human, I'd say she was in a self-induced coma. She has all the signs of it. But since this is Miss Wiles we are talking about," he paused, but since I couldn't see him didn't know what he was doing until he started speaking again, "From my short experience, Miss Wiles will wake up when her body is ready. Right now, I am doing all I can to keep them from running any blood work on her. We don't want another incident like before," he chuckled but it sounded strained.

"Thanks Doc," Trisha sighed, "I guess I'll just have to wait and see."

Doctor Ryan asked her something but I didn't catch it because my world became black once more.

The next time I woke I could move my mouth. My lips were dry and I flicked my tongue out to lick them. Just moving such a small number of muscles was excruciating.

The beeping of the monitors hooked to me were the only sound in the room, the annoying bleep-bleep of my heart monitor making me want to scream. For the first time, I prayed for the darkness to take me once more.

Thankfully, not long after, it did.

My nose itched. Torturously so. I tried to lift my arm, but it could have been a Mack truck for how heavy it felt.

I wiggled my nose in an attempt to ease the itch, but it didn't help much. I found I could move my head and tried desperately to rub my face against my shoulder. Sadly, my shoulder was having none of it and would not lift enough to meet my face.

I flopped my head back onto the pillow beneath my head and groaned.

The noise alerted someone, because a rush of footsteps pounded the floor. A swish and then a brush of air flittered across my face. I tried once more to open my lids and found they weren't quite as heavy as before. I peeked through my lashes to see a very worried Trisha at my side.

"Hey," I moved my lips but no sounds came out. I coughed and licked my lips. Trisha rushed to grab a cup of water and offered the straw to me.

I sipped it slowly not trusting my ability to swallow without choking. When I was done, I heaved a big sigh and then tried again.

"How long?"

"How long have you been out?" Trisha sat on the edge of the bed, her outfit mild for her tastes. Black jeans and a worn-out metal band shirt. Her hair tied up in a messy bun. I knew it couldn't have gotten too bad because her makeup was in perfect condition.

"Yeah."

Trisha smiled slightly and took my hand in hers. "Long enough to freak everyone out."

I narrowed my already slitted eyes at her, making myself almost blind. It didn't have the desired effect and only cause Trisha to laugh.

"Only you could look so peeved while in a hospital bed," when I only stared at her in response, she held her hands up, "Okay, okay. But don't get mad at me."

"Trisha," I warned. Her elusiveness to my simple question started to worry me.

"Three months."

My eyes bugged out of my head and I forced myself to move. The shift of muscles and bones shot sharp needles of pain through every nerve. Trisha reached out to stop me, easily pushing me back onto the bed. She pressed a button on the side of the bed, and it began to rise to a sitting position, but even that movement pained me.

"Three months?" I asked in disbelief, "Are you sure?"

Trisha gave me an incredulous look, "Of course I'm sure. I've spent the last three months running your business and moving your things." she ticked them off on her fingers, "and then there was the funeral for Madame Serena—which you missed by the way." She shot me an apologetic look.

Three months. Trying to use my powers on Asmodeus and killing Ramiel instead had cost me three months. If I had known Ramiel had that much devotion to the demon lord I wouldn't have even tried it. But now Ramiel was dead, Asmodeus had the blade and probably Sid too in hell. While I was stuck in this damn bed. Anger and frustration caused my eyes to prickle with tears.

"Hey," Trisha shushed, rubbing my hand, "Don't worry. No one cares you missed it. They know you were here."

I growled and used as much strength as I could muster to pull my arm away. "I'm not upset about that."

"Then, what is it?" Trisha frowned, "Is it about me moving your stuff? 'Cause I assumed you'd want to move-"

"Why'd you move my stuff?" I asked, confusion replacing my anger. "Did we get kicked out of the building?"

Trisha laughed and waved a hand, "No, no. We didn't get evicted. Madame Serena actually left you the deed to the whole thing."

"She what?"

"Madame Serena left you the building in her will. Well," Trisha paused, and then said, "Technically the building belonged to the guild, but the official record says it goes to you. So, I figured you'd want to move the main office to the bottom floor and then the top floor would be all yours."

"I don't need all that space, though." I still wasn't comprehending all she was saying. I owned the building? The whole building? What the heck would I do with the whole building?

Trisha scoffed, "Well, you might not need it, but I sure as hell do. I'm tired of only having a crummy little waiting area. Now we can renovate it into a whole new fancy place."

"There's the still issue of money," I reminded her, thinking it would bring her back to reality. But my words only made her grin widen.

"With the big fat check you got from the FBI," she wiggled her eyebrows up and down.

"For what?"

"Services rendered of course. For helping them catch a serial killer," she answered as if I should know.

"But that was just a bunch of bull crap the guild made up," I countered. Things were going in too good of a direction. There had to be a catch.

Trisha sighed in frustration, "Technically you did stop a serial killer. Asmodeus was killing women as he always does, but this time he had been picking off witches and the like. Probably trying to get the charm off him. So, Adara's dad wasn't really lying when he'd said the FBI had a case open, because they had already started one. They just threw Madame Serena in with his victims."

I frowned hard at this information. To an outsider, Madame Serena had been one of the other victims, but why Ramiel had killed her I couldn't understand. There was so many other things he could have done to stop her from helping me, but I guess now I would never know.

A part of me was saddened. I had never meant to use my powers on him, but he had jumped in front of Asmodeus. He had made his choice and there was nothing I could do about it.

Ramiel's decisions and Madame Serena's death aside, I wasn't humble enough to say no to free money. With all that had been going on I hadn't been paying much attention to my business. The fact that I even still had one—considering I'd been out for three months—surprised me.

Doctor Ryan stepped in then interrupting my thoughts. "Ah, Miss Wiles. Happy to see you awake. How are you feeling?"

"Like I broke every bone in my body," I winced and settled against the pillows once more.

He gave me a small smile, "Well, I can assure you all of your bones are intact and on the outwardly you are in fit condition," he looked down at his file and then met my gaze, "But then again, I presume it wasn't your body that needed healing."

"No," I agreed, "I suppose not."

"We're going to keep you for a few more days. At least, until you can move around in your own. Do you have an issue with that?"

I shook my head, and then promptly stopped as a wave of nausea came over me. "That's fine. I don't have anywhere I need to be."

"Alright, I'll get your chart updated and you," he pointed at Trisha, "don't start badgering her with work."

"Wouldn't dare," Trisha swore with a raised hand, an innocent expression on her face.

After Doctor Ryan left, I glanced at Trisha. "How's it looking on the portal front? Did you guys find someone to open one?"

Trisha frowned and then chewed on her bottom lip, "Apparently, high-level sorcerers are hard to find. Adara tried to get the guild to help but they are refusing to. The demons are where they belong," she said it in a deep mocking voice, which led me to believe she'd been there when it had been decided.

"There's something else," Trisha said, her voice changing to a cautious sort. I waited for her to continue, not wanting to assume anything, "Your friend, Uriel, came by."

"Uriel?" my eyes widened at my fellow angel's name, "What did she want?"

Trisha's face held an array of emotions. She seemed conflicted about telling me what Uriel had to say. Eventually, she said, "She said she had asked around about Michael's blade. No one knew how to destroy it, but they did know something else about it," she hesitated and shifted slightly, "The blade doesn't just open portals to hell. It can also open portals to heaven."

I heard Trisha's words, but it was as if all the blood had rushed to my head. Everything became muffled and only the pounding of my heart could be heard. When I was finally able to calm myself down, Trisha was shaking me.

"Mary, did you hear me?" her voice almost shrill, "If you get the dagger back, you can go home."

About the Author

Erin Bedford is a *USA Today* bestselling fantasy and paranormal romance author, a computer programmer by day, and a hobby hoarder.

Creating fantastical worlds have always been a secret passion of hers and she couldn't imagine writing any story without some kind of lovey-dovey or smexy goodness in it.

Read More from Erin Bedford

www.erinbedford.com

www.ingramcontent.com/pod-product-compliance
Lightning Source LLC
Chambersburg PA
CBHW070920190726
48292CB00004B/1043